Oregon
Oceanauts

"Ever since you came to my school, everyone has been addicted to your books! My teacher is reading one to us right now, and it's great!"

-Mark F., age 11, Kentucky

"You need to put more pictures of your dogs on your website. I think they're super cute."

-Michelle H., age 12, Oregon

"I have read every one of your American Chillers and Michigan Chillers books. The best one was WICKED VELO-CIRAPTORS OF WEST VIRGINIA. That book gave me nightmares!"

-Erik M., age 9, Florida

"How do you come up with so many cool ideas for your books? You write some really freaky stuff, and that's good."

-Heather G., age 8, Maryland

"I met you at your store, Chillermania, last year. Thanks for signing my books for me! It was the best part of our vacation!"

-David L., age 13, Illinois

"A couple of years ago, I was too young to read your books and they scared me. Now, I love them! I read them every day!"

-Alex P., age 8, Minnesota

"I love your books, and I love to write. My dream is to come to AUTHOR QUEST when I'm old enough. My mom says I can, if I get accepted. I hope I can be a great writer, just like you!"

-Cynthia W., age 8, South Dakota

"Everyone loved it when you came to our school and did an assembly. You were really funny, and we learned a lot about writing and reading."

-Chad R., age 10, Arizona

"You are my favorite author in the whole world! I love every single one of your books!"

-Amy P., age 9, Michigan

"I heard that you wear those weird glasses when you write your books. Is that true? If it is, keep wearing them. Your books are cool!"

-Griffin W., age 12, Maine

"HAUNTING IN NEW HAMPSHIRE is the best ghost story ever! EVER!"

-Kaylee J., age 11, Tennessee

"I don't think anyone else in the world could write as good as you! My favorite book is NEBRASKA NIGHTCRAWL-ERS. Britney is just like me."

-Taylor, M., age 10, Michigan

"I used to hate to read, and now I love it, because of your books. They're really cool! When I read, I pretend that I'm the main character, and I always get freaked out."

-Jack C., age 9, Colorado

Got something cool to say about Johnathan Rand's books? Let us know, and we might publish it right here! Send your short blurb to:
Chiller Blurbs
281 Cool Blurbs Ave.
Topinabee, MI 49791

Other books by Johnathan Rand:

Michigan Chillers:

American Chillers:

Freddie Fernortner, Fearless First Grader:

Adventure Club series:

For Teens:

PANDEMIA: A novel of the bird flu and the end of the world
(written with Christopher Knight)

American Chillers Double Thrillers:

Vampire Nation &
Attack of the Monster Venus Melon

AMERICAN CHILLERS

America's #1 Series for MAXIMUM Chills!

#29:
Oregon
Oceanauts

Johnathan Rand

An AudioCraft Publishing, Inc. book

Book storage and warehouses provided by Chillermania!©
Indian River, Michigan

American Chillers #29: Oregon Oceanauts
ISBN 13-digit: 978-1-893699-24-3

Librarians/Media Specialists:
PCIP/MARC records available **free of charge** at
www.americanchillers.com

Cover illustration by Dwayne Harris
Cover layout and design by Sue Harring

Dickinson Press Inc., Grand Rapids MI, USA • Job 3762300 September 2010

OREGON
OCEANAUTS

VISIT CHILLERMANIA!

WORLD HEADQUARTERS FOR BOOKS BY JOHNATHAN RAND!

CHILLERMANIA!

**I-75 Exit 313
then south
1 mile!**

Visit the HOME for books by Johnathan Rand! Featuring books, hats, shirts, bookmarks and other cool stuff not available anywhere else in the world! Plus, watch the American Chillers website for news of special events and signings at *CHILLERMANIA!* with author Johnathan Rand! Located in northern lower Michigan, on I-75! Take exit 313 . . . then south 1 mile! For more info, call (231) 238-0338. And be afraid! Be veeeery afraaaaaaiiiid . . . .

1

As I gazed out over the choppy sea, emotions swept over me like the waves churning before my eyes. I was nervous, and I'm not a bit ashamed to admit I was a little afraid. After all: what we were about to do was risky and dangerous.

But it had to be done. We had to succeed. If we didn't, the ocean would face a terrible environmental disaster.

There were two of us that would play an important role in the mission: me and my younger sister, Shannon. She was seated next to me on the boat as it bobbed up and down in the sea. Above, the sun glowed like a lemon drop in the blue sky. Below, glittering diamonds reflected off the choppy sea. The only sounds were the wind in my ears and the water lapping at the side of the *Sea Falcon,* the big research boat we were on. Several other vessels were moored nearby.

"How long, Jacob?" Shannon asked.

"I don't know," I replied. "But I'm sure we'll be suiting up soon."

On the deck in front of us, our gear was in two piles: wetsuits, vests, air tanks, and various tools we would need to complete our mission. We didn't want to suit up until we were ready to dive, as being in a wetsuit in the hot sun would cause us to bake. We were waiting for word from the mission specialists that the dive was a go.

Finally, one of the scientists came up from below and told us it was time. We suited up in silence with the help of two laboratory technicians. They were very professional and knew what they were doing. And they treated us like adults, not kids. I liked that. What we were doing was important, and if it could have been done by adults, it would have been.

But it couldn't. The mission required small

people—kids—to perform the dangerous tasks at the bottom of the ocean. Sound crazy? That's what I thought . . . at first.

After we'd donned our wetsuits, checked our air tanks, and performed other necessary tests, we were ready.

And I really thought we would succeed. I thought we would be heroes.

But as Shannon and I slipped backward off the boat and into the crystal blue water, I had no idea of the horrors waiting for us in the murky depths of the Pacific Ocean.

2

For you to understand what's going on, I need to go back to where everything began. On May ninth of this year, I was a pretty typical kid leading a pretty typical life. I went to school, did my homework (most of the time), played pranks on my sister, and played basketball with my friends.

But that night, I saw something that was soon to change my life and lead to a series of adventures most kids my age don't get to have.

My sister, my mom, and I live in Portland, a city

in the very northern region of the state of Oregon, bordering Washington. In fact, we live so close to Washington that I can ride my bicycle there. Not many other kids in the country could say they do that.

Where we live is really cool. Portland is the biggest city in the state. Summers are great; it's sunny and warm. In the winter, we get a lot of rain, but hardly any snow, because it doesn't stay cold long enough. And Portland is the home of the Portland Trail Blazers, my favorite basketball team. That used to be my favorite sport—basketball. But not anymore. You see, I've since discovered a new sport. A sport I love more than basketball or any other sport: scuba diving.

I'd already known what scuba diving was, as I'd seen shows on television showing men and women dressed in wetsuits and special gear, staying under water for long periods of time, breathing air through a mouthpiece called a regulator that connected to a hose that was affixed to a tank on their backs. I thought it was pretty cool, but I never imagined myself ever doing anything like that. After all: I was just a kid, and I'd never seen kids scuba diving on television before, and figured there was some sort of age limit.

I was surfing through the channels on TV when

my sister, Shannon, came into the room. Shannon is eleven—one year younger than me. We get along pretty well, but I play pranks on her sometimes and she gets mad at me. Once, I put a plastic spider under the covers in her bed. When she found it later that night, she totally freaked out. She thought it was real and screamed her head off. Mom ran into the room, worried. And I got in trouble! I was grounded for a week and couldn't go out of the house, except when I went to school.

"What are you watching?" Shannon said as she sat on the other end of the couch.

"Nothing yet," I replied.

I scanned the channels, searching for something fun to watch.

Finally, something interesting appeared on the screen: a man scuba diving. All around him, a school of fish hung in the blue-green water, swirling like colorful clouds. The fish weren't scared of him at all. They swarmed around him, more curious than frightened. It was mesmerizing to watch the man move in slow motion in the water, with shiny bubbles of air emerging from his mouthpiece and rising to the surface.

"Hey, that's cool," Shannon said. "Leave it on that channel."

I put the remote on the armrest and sat back to watch. The scuba diver hung in the water, motionless, watching fish of all sizes swirl around him.

"I'd like to do that," Shannon said.

Me, too, I thought. But I knew it would never happen. You see, I'm very small for my age. Shannon is, too. When I play basketball, I'm not very good at shooting or getting rebounds, because I'm so short. But I have one great advantage: because I'm small, I can move very, very fast . . . much faster than anyone else in my grade. When I play basketball with my friends, everyone wants me on their team because I'm so quick. I'm also pretty good at dodgeball, soccer, and other sports where you have to move fast.

But I was certain that when it came to scuba diving, I wouldn't be able to do it until I got bigger. I figured the air tank alone probably weighed more than I did, and I'd never be able to carry it on my back.

It will be years before I'll be able to take a course and learn to scuba dive, I thought. *In fact, I will probably—*

And that's when my thought was interrupted by

a horrific sound of crashing metal and breaking glass on the street in front of our house.

3

Shannon and I leapt from the couch and turned, looking out the big window facing our front yard. In the street, two cars had collided, and both front ends were a mangled mess. The vehicle on the left was a white car. Its hood was crinkled like an accordion, and gray smoke boiled up from the engine.

The other vehicle was a van. The front of it was smashed in, and the windshield had shattered. Tiny particles of glass were sprinkled on the road.

"Call nine-one-one!" I shouted to Shannon. She

raced to grab the phone while I ran out of the living room, through the front door, and across the yard.

What if someone is hurt? I wondered. My thoughts were frantic, my mind anxious. *If someone is hurt badly, I don't know what to do.*

Thankfully, a woman was getting out of the white car. It appeared she was the only one inside, and it didn't seem like she was hurt.

But the man in the van had a bloody nose. As he opened the door, I could see that the vehicle's air bag had deployed. Now it was deflated, and it crumpled over the hood like a battered circus balloon.

"Are you all right?" I asked as I approached. Which was kind of a silly question, being that I could see blood running from his nose, over his mouth, and onto his chin.

"I think I'm fine," the man said, "except for this." And with that, he placed his thumb and forefinger to his nose, closing his nostrils to stem the flow of blood. "When the air bag went off, it knocked my fist into my face. I gave myself a bloody nose."

"I'll get you a towel!" I said, and I spun and ran into the house. In the living room, Shannon was on the phone talking to the emergency operator, giving the person details about the accident. I ran past her, turned, and went down the hall and into the bathroom.

A cold, wet towel, I thought. *That would probably help.*

Without thinking, I grabbed one of Mom's good towels—the ones we aren't supposed to use—that was hanging from the rack. She says they match the curtains, and they're only for decoration . . . which is kind of silly, if you ask me. After all: what good is a towel hanging on the rack if you can't use it?

I ran the cold water for a moment, then soaked the towel and wrung it out. I ran down the hall and through the living room, where Shannon had just ended her phone call.

"The lady said she was sending someone right away," she said. "Is that guy hurt bad?"

"I think it's just a bloody nose," I said as I darted out the front door. Shannon followed as I sprinted across the lawn.

The woman that had been driving the white car was near the curb, talking on a small phone. The man was sitting on the sidewalk, still holding his nose, when I approached. Other neighbors, alerted by the crash, were coming out of their houses.

"Here," I said to the man, and I held out the cold, wet towel.

"Thanks," he said. He balled the towel around his nose and tipped his head back. "I haven't had a bloody nose in years," he said. "Once, I fell forward in a boat and couldn't catch myself. Smacked myself a good one and broke my nose."

In the distance, I heard a siren.

"Help is coming," Shannon said. "I just called nine-one-one."

"Thank you," the man said, still holding his head back. "I think I'm going to be okay. Looks like we were both lucky this time."

He was right. As it turned out, the woman's car had a broken tie rod. While I don't really know what that is, my mom later told me it controls the car's steering. When the tie rod broke, the woman lost control and swerved into the man's oncoming van.

I thought Mom was going to be mad at me for using one of her good towels, but she wasn't. She said she was glad we acted fast and did the right thing. Mom said she was proud of both Shannon and me, saying we'd done the right things when it really mattered.

I didn't really think I'd done anything that important. I mean, all I did was get a towel for the guy. Shannon called nine-one-one. Nobody was hurt badly, and neither the woman nor the man had to be taken to the hospital. Two wreckers came, cleaned the street, and hauled away the two crippled vehicles. Mom took us out for pizza and ice cream, and we went home.

A week later, I'd forgotten all about the accident . . . until a letter addressed to Shannon and me came in the mail one afternoon.

4

I had been playing basketball with my friends at the park. The day was sunny and hot, and around five o'clock, our teams broke up. Most of us had to go home to get cleaned up and ready for dinner.

When I walked into the house, Mom was on the phone. She held her finger to her lips, indicating I should be silent.

"Yes," she was saying, "that's right. And if you—"

I didn't pay any more attention to what she was

saying, because Mom picked up a letter that was on the couch, smiled, and handed it to me while she talked on the phone.

I took the letter. It was addressed to me and Shannon. In the upper-left hand corner, there was a small cartoon character—a scuba diver. Beneath it were the words *Waters of Wonder Scuba Shop*.

I frowned. *Why would Shannon and I get a letter from a scuba shop?*

Strange.

I opened the letter, not sure what to expect. It contained a handwritten letter in blue ink. I unfolded the paper and read.

Dear Jacob and Shannon:

I contacted the police department to get your names and address so I could send a letter of thanks. Last week, I was involved in a car crash on your street. You two helped out by bringing me a towel and contacting the authorities.

Although my injury was minor, I deeply appreciate both of you coming to my assistance, and I would like to repay you. I am the owner of Waters of Wonder Scuba Shop, and I would like to offer both of you free scuba diving lessons. The course begins next week and lasts for one month. Classes will be held in the classroom and the pool at my shop, and your final test for certification will take place in the ocean.

I was trembling with excitement. I continued to read the letter.

Please let me know at your earliest convenience. There will be others taking the scuba class, and I'll need to reserve the spaces for both of you.

Again, thank you for your help. You might be happy to know that my nose is going to be fine, although it's still a little purple and swollen.

Sincerely,

Morris Lukeman

My mouth hung open as I read the letter over.

Scuba diving lessons? I thought. *Free? But what about my age? What about my size? Didn't that matter?*

Mr. Lukeman obviously knew how big Shannon and I were.

He must think we're big enough, I thought. *Maybe it doesn't matter how big I am, after all.*

Mom hung up the phone. She saw my surprised expression and smiled.

"Who's the letter from?" she asked.

"The guy we helped last week!" I blurted,

waving the letter in the air. "He wants to give me and Shannon free scuba lessons!"

I gave her the letter to read, just as Shannon strode through the front door.

"Shannon!" I said. "You're not going to believe this, but that guy says we can take scuba lessons for free!"

"What guy?" Shannon said.

"The guy in the car accident last week! He owns a scuba diving shop, and he wants to thank us by giving us free scuba diving lessons!"

"That's awesome!" Shannon exclaimed.

"This is very nice of him," Mom said when she'd finished reading the letter.

"Let me see," Shannon said, and she held out her hand and took the letter from Mom.

"Can we?" I asked.

Mom shrugged. "I don't see why not," she said. "It sounds like a fun adventure for the both of you."

Oh, it would be an adventure, all right.

An adventure . . . into disaster.

5

Class began on Thursday the following week. There would be two classes each week for a month, during which we would study from books, take tests and quizzes, watch videos, and learn everything there is to know about scuba diving. The class ended with an open water test, when we would go scuba diving in the ocean with Mr. Lukeman. He would grade us on how we did.

I was so excited I couldn't stand it! Ever since we received the letter and Mom said we could take the class, it was the only thing I thought about. Shannon and I went to the library and checked out books about scuba diving. We visited websites and watched videos. We wanted to learn as much as we could before class started. I learned that the word 'scuba' was actually the acronym for 'Self-Contained Underwater Breathing Apparatus.' Neither Shannon nor I knew that before.

I had wondered if scuba diving was dangerous. As it turns out, I found that more people were injured while wearing their gear on land or in a boat, because it's difficult and clumsy to move around while carrying all the bulky, added weight. Scuba diving, when done properly, is a safe sport.

Still, like any sport, scuba diving has its risks, and it was important to know what could go wrong and how to prevent problems.

I also found out that scuba diving can be enjoyed by just about anyone, and it doesn't matter how old or how big you are. I don't think a little kid could scuba dive, but I discovered there are many people my age and even younger who are certified and enjoy diving.

The class was fun. Twelve people attended. Shannon and I were the only kids in the class; the rest were adults.

We were all assigned 'buddies.' Shannon was my buddy. That was a primary rule of scuba diving: never dive alone. Always have a buddy. That way, if you get into trouble, your buddy will be there to help.

And the classes were a lot of work. Not only was there a lot of reading and studying to do, but we had homework . . . just like school. There were tests and quizzes that required a lot of thought. Scuba diving isn't anything like swimming in a pool or lake, that's for sure.

But I did very well, and so did Shannon. We studied hard, learned a lot, and aced the quizzes and tests. We practiced diving in the pool, which was a lot of fun. There wasn't much to look at, but it was cool anyway. It was exciting to put on all of the equipment for the very first time and even more exciting to dip beneath the surface of the water.

Mr. Lukeman turned out to be a great teacher and a really nice guy. He'd been scuba diving for forty years, and he was very experienced. He told us stories about how he'd explored shipwrecks on the bottom of the ocean and how he traveled to Michigan to dive the Great Lakes in search of ships lost long ago.

Finally, the classes and quizzes were over, and it was time for our final test: an open water dive. We were going to drive to a beach on the western coast of Oregon and make our dives in the Pacific Ocean. Mom, Shannon, and I had swam in the ocean before, and we usually drive over to the coast a couple of times every summer for a picnic. It's only about an hour's drive from home. We always have a great time.

But today was different. I was excited, sure. But I was also a little nervous. Who wouldn't be? It was an important day. I told myself I was ready, I was prepared, that I would pass with flying colors.

But as we were about to find out, there are some things you just can't prepare for.

6

We drove to the ocean in several vehicles. Mom took us in her car, while a few other members of the class rode in a van driven by Mr. Lukeman. There was also another worker from the dive shop who brought an underwater camera, so he could take pictures of us in the ocean.

"I'm so excited, I can't stand it," Shannon said from the back seat. I was sitting in the front, next to Mom, reading my dive manual, studying everything, going over dive tables and charts. I wanted to be sure

I was ready for our open water test.

"I am, too," I said. "I've been waiting for this day ever since class started."

"I think I'm just as excited as you two," Mom said. "Maybe I'll take scuba diving lessons, too. That way, we can take a scuba diving vacation together."

"Really?!?!" I said. "That would be awesome!"

"Yeah, Mom!" Shannon said, leaping forward in her seat. "We could go to some tropical island and dive the coral reefs!"

My mind was spinning with a billion possibilities.

Think of all the cool adventures we could have! I thought. *We could hunt for shipwrecks and explore all sorts of cool places!*

Finally, we arrived at the beach. The day was perfect. The sun was out, and the air and water were warm. The waves were small, too, which would make our dive even easier. Mr. Lukeman said if the waves were too big, we'd have to postpone the dive.

Another van carrying our equipment arrived. Everyone helped unload the gear and gather it in piles on beach towels. The equipment didn't belong to us; Mr. Lukeman was loaning it to us. I thought it would be cool to have my very own stuff, but I'd have to save a lot of money before I bought my own equipment.

At the beach, Mr. Lukeman gave us some last minute instructions, but it seemed like I'd heard his talk a thousand times. I had paid attention in class, studied, and read. I was ready. We all were.

"Are there any questions?" Mr. Lukeman asked.

No one raised their hands.

"Good," he said with a smile. "Time to suit up. Carry your fins to the water before you put them on."

The moment we'd waited for had arrived: our first open water dive, our final test before our certification. We all knew what to do, we all knew what to expect.

What we didn't know, however, was that something was waiting for us, cruising just beneath the surface, unknown and unseen.

7

Shannon and I put our gear on. First was the wetsuit, followed by booties, gloves, and a hood, all made from foamed neoprene. The suit serves many purposes. The deeper you dive, the colder it gets. A wetsuit helps keep a diver warm, and it also serves as protection against cuts and scratches.

Then came our weight belts. These are usually made of lead and often wrapped in nylon. Divers need weight belts to help them sink, because a wetsuit is very buoyant. If you wear a full wetsuit without anything else, you'll float like a cork, and it will be nearly impossible to swim beneath the surface. A weight belt worn around the waist helps counteract the buoyancy of the wetsuit.

I put my mask on, but I kept the glass lens over my head until I was ready to dive.

Then, I checked my air tank, making sure it was full. Before connecting the regulator hose, I turned the air on for a quick burst, just to make sure air was flowing through the hose.

After connecting the hose to the tank, I took a breath through the regulator. It was working fine.

"Can you help me get into my BC vest?" Shannon asked. BC stands for 'buoyancy control,' and the vest is made especially for scuba diving. Not only does it serve as a harness for the air tank, but it also holds air like a balloon. When you inflate the vest, it's easy to float in the water, even with an air tank and a weight belt. As a diver lets the air out of the vest through a small nozzle, he becomes less buoyant and begins to sink. The vest aids a diver in becoming what is called 'neutrally buoyant,' which means he neither sinks nor rises in the water, making moving around in the water less work.

I picked up Shannon's vest and helped her put it on, then she did the same for me. The vest doesn't weigh much, but when the air tank is affixed to it, it is heavy.

While we suited up, Mom stood a few feet away, taking pictures.

"You both look so cute," she kept saying. "Wait until I send these pictures to your grandparents."

I rolled my eyes and checked over my gear.

Everyone in the class was ready. Together, we walked to the water, where we put on our fins. Then, we walked backward through the small waves, because it's easier to walk that way while wearing fins. As soon as I was up to my waist, I turned and slunk forward, settling into the water, swimming.

My first glimpse beneath the surface was magical. I'd never swam in a lake or ocean with a mask before. My first and only experiences had been in Mr. Lukeman's pool, which is *nothing* like the open water.

I was amazed with what I saw: a sandy ocean floor, my bright yellow fins, and a few small, colorful fish that skirted away. Shannon was on my left, and the rest of the class was close by as we slowly swam along the surface, heading out to deeper water. Mr.

Lukeman led our group, and soon, we were in water over our heads.

He paused and the rest of the class stopped, bobbing in the water, our floatation aided by our BC vests.

Mr. Lukeman bobbed in the water, glancing at everyone. He nodded and smiled at me and Shannon, then pulled the regulator from his mouth.

"Everybody ready?" he asked.

We all raised a gloved hand and touched our forefingers with our thumbs, which is the 'all-okay' sign for divers.

"Good!" he said. "Stay with your buddies, and let's begin the dive."

I looked at Shannon. Of course, the only thing I could see were her eyes through the lens of her mask, but I could tell that even with the regulator in her mouth, she was smiling. She was just as excited as I was.

I pressed the lever on my vest to release air. As it seeped out, I sank lower and lower in the water. Soon, my head was beneath the surface, and I was breathing comfortably through my regulator. Around me, Shannon and the other divers were doing the same.

I was excited, but I remained calm. That's one thing that's very important while scuba diving: remain calm. Getting exited or anxious causes you to breathe harder and faster, wasting air. It will also tire you out faster, and scuba diving shouldn't be strenuous. It should be a smooth, relaxing experience.

Another thing I really liked was the silence. Beneath the surface, it's very quiet. The only thing I could hear was the sound of my own breathing and the bubbles from my exhaled air leaving my regulator and rising to the surface.

The group continued swimming just a few feet above the sandy bottom. I saw dozens of colorful shells and rocks. Curious fish darted away. The water was blue-green and very clear.

Ahead of us, Mr. Lukeman stopped and stood on the sandy bottom, just like he would stand on the beach. His fins created a small dust storm of swirling sand as he looked around at his class. Then, he raised his right hand and made a fist, which was our signal to grasp one hand with our assigned buddy and raise it above our heads.

I grasped Shannon's hand and held it up. Others

in the group did the same.

I'm really doing it! I thought, and I remembered back to the television show I'd watched, thinking that it would be a long time before I'd be able to scuba dive.

In addition to the regulator hose, there was another hose attached to my tank. This had a fist-sized gauge at the end of it that gave me a reading of how much air was left in the tank and what depth we were at. Currently, we were in twenty-five feet of water.

Too cool, I thought.

I tilted my head back up to see what the surface looked like, but I was shocked to see an enormous, dark shadow, easily ten feet long. Instantly, I knew what it was, and in the same instant, horror swept through my entire body.

Cruising above us was an enormous shark!

8

I know that one of the first rules of scuba diving is to stay calm . . . but that's a hard thing to do when a man-eating fish is swimming only a few feet above your head.

I waved my arm frantically to get the attention of Mr. Lukeman. Then, I pointed up at the shark, where I then saw something else: another diver. He and the shark were slowly descending toward the group. The diver had been on the other side of the shark, and I hadn't seen him. Now that they were closer, I could see the shark wasn't alive after all. It was fake, and it must have been made with plastic or something so it would sink. Still, it looked very real, very lifelike. The diver had a hold of the tail, and was pulling it with him.

What's he doing with a fake shark? I wondered.

Soon, I realized what was happening. Another worker from the dive shop produced an underwater camera, and all of us in the class took turns posing with the 'shark' with our buddies. Later, it would be a cool souvenir to remember our very first open water dive.

The dive was exciting, and nothing went wrong. The class spread out a little, but we remained pretty much together as we explored the watery depths. There wasn't too much to see—a few shells, some fish—things like that. Mr. Lukeman had told us that our first dive wasn't going to be about sightseeing, but about training and underwater safety and to help us get acquainted with the undersea world. Soon, he said, we could take guided trips to explore different parts of the sea.

And in the following weeks, that's what Shannon and I did: we signed up for scuba diving trips at Mr. Lukeman's dive shop. Some of them were conducted by Mr. Lukeman, while others were led by other workers at the shop. Most of the time, the trips were in the ocean, and we'd travel to different places by boat. Mr. Lukeman and others commented that Shannon and I were quickly becoming very skillful scuba divers, and it made me proud.

Until one hot, July afternoon when disaster struck.

9

We were diving in relatively shallow water—around thirty feet deep—exploring the remains of an old ship. There really wasn't much to see. The ship had sank hundreds of years ago and had disintegrated into nothing more than a pile of boards scattered on the sea floor, covered with layers of fine, coarse silt and vegetation. Mr. Lukeman had discovered the wreck by accident, only a mile from the shore.

On this particular day, there were eight of us, including the captain of the boat, who remained on board and didn't dive.

The eight of us were cruising a few feet above the bottom, inspecting the remains of the ship. It was the first wreck Shannon and I had visited, and although the remains looked nothing at all like a ship, it was still fun and exciting.

By then, Shannon and I were as comfortable in the water as we were on land. We'd completed dozens of dives. Usually, a guided dive trip costs money, but Mr. Lukeman told us that if we agreed to work around the shop doing odd jobs, we could rent dive equipment and go on dive trips in exchange. We did all sorts of things: mowed the lawn around the shop, washed windows, cleaned the pool, and ran errands for Mr. Lukeman or other staff members. We even helped out with customers, as we were becoming more and more familiar with dive equipment and the scuba business, just from hanging out at the shop so much.

And Mom liked the fact that Shannon and I had found a hobby we could do together. She didn't even have to take us to the dive shop, because it was only a mile away and we rode our bikes there.

Still, I dreamed of having my own equipment, my own vest and my own tank. I was saving money I earned doing other odd jobs around the neighborhood, in hopes of earning enough to buy my own mask, snorkel, and fins. That way, I could still experience the undersea world . . . although I wouldn't be able to remain beneath the surface for long, because I wouldn't have an air tank.

Secretly, I dreamed about working as an actual, full-time employee at *Waters of Wonder Scuba Shop*, working for Mr. Lukeman in the store, and maybe even taking divers on guided tours myself.

And that's what I was thinking about as Shannon and I moved slowly over the old wreck: growing up and having my own equipment, traveling the world, scuba diving all over the place. It would be an exciting, adventurous life.

Beneath us, there were several old boards with jagged pieces of rusty metal sticking up. Like Mr. Lukeman had told us, the wreck was so decayed that it looked nothing at all like a ship.

Shannon descended deeper, reaching out to fan the water and swirl away some of the silt that had gathered on one of the boards.

Unfortunately, she wasn't being careful. Her regulator hose brushed against one of the pieces of metal. Although it was rusty, it was very sharp, and it sliced Shannon's regulator hose in two.

Air bubbles poured from the hose and spiraled to the surface as the contents of Shannon's tank spilled out wildly, uncontrolled. Through her mask, I saw her eyes, wide and horror-filled.

We were at the bottom of the sea . . . and Shannon had no way to breathe.

10

It was time for all of my training, for all of my preparation to pay off. My sister's life depended on it.

Instantly, I knew that what I *wouldn't* do was more important than what I *would* do.

I *wouldn't* panic.

If I panicked, it would just create more trouble.

And it was important for Shannon not to panic, too. Sure, I knew she was scared. But she needed to keep a clear head about things. If she did, she would be okay.

The first thing she did was place her hand to her neck, making a sawing motion. This was the diver's universal signal that he was out of air.

I descended to her, took a breath, then pulled the regulator from my mouth. Shannon removed the useless regulator from her own mouth and took my regulator in her other hand. While I held my breath, she placed it in her mouth and took a breath, then exhaled, then took another breath. She handed the regulator back to me, and I returned it to my mouth and breathed for a moment. This is called 'buddy breathing,' and it's a technique we had practiced in the pool during training.

Meanwhile, air bubbles continued to spew from the damaged regulator hose, rising and swirling like silvery, shimmering balloons. It wouldn't be long before her tank was completely empty.

Shannon gave me the 'all okay' signal with her thumb and forefinger; I gave her the same signal back, then pointed to the surface. Although things really weren't 'all okay,' we knew we could overcome the situation we were in. We ascended together, slowly and calmly, buddy breathing until we reached the surface.

Two other divers had spotted us and swam alongside. They could see our problem and ascended next to us, just in case we needed help.

Thankfully, we made it to the surface without any difficulty. There was still enough air in Shannon's tank to inflate her vest, and we both bobbed easily in the water. I pulled my mask to my forehead, and Shannon did the same.

"Are you all right?" I asked.

"Yeah," Shannon replied. "I sure was scared, though. When I breathed in and got a mouthful of water, I knew I was in trouble."

"You didn't panic," I said. "That's the main thing."

And I know this might sound funny, but I was really proud of my sister at that moment. Here was a girl who screamed bloody murder when I hid in her closet and leapt out to scare her. Yet, when she'd been faced with a life-threatening situation, all of her emergency training had kicked into gear. She stayed cool and calm in the face of danger and lived to tell about it. I, too, hadn't panicked and had been able to help my sister.

As it was, it was good practice. Soon, all of our

emergency training skills were going to be put to the test. Not tests like what we had in our classes, either. These would be *real* tests where failure wouldn't mean receiving a bad grade . . . failure would mean the ultimate penalty: death.

11

We continued diving through the fall, until the weather soured and grew cold. During the winter months, there were many dive trips scheduled for warmer, tropical waters—Bermuda, Belize, the Cayman Islands—but we certainly didn't have the money to do that. Mom said maybe in the future we could, but I thought it was unlikely. Mom worked hard as it was, and we still didn't have a lot of money . . . certainly not enough for all of us to go on a tropical diving vacation.

So, while I wasn't diving, I read scuba diving

magazines and worked at Mr. Lukeman's store. He paid me money, and I opened an account at a nearby bank. I saved every penny, in hopes of saving enough money over the winter months to buy some scuba equipment in the spring. Going to school and working at the dive shop, the months flew by.

One morning in early April, just after seven, the phone rang. Shannon and I were in the kitchen, eating cereal, and Mom was getting ready for work.

"I'll get it," I said, and I stood and walked to the phone hanging on the wall. The caller ID displayed Mr. Lukeman's name.

"Hi, Mr. Lukeman," I said as I pressed the receiver to my ear. But all along I was wondering: *Why is he calling at such an early hour?*

"Good morning, Jacob," he said. His voice was heavy, somber. He sounded concerned. "I need to speak with you and your sister," he continued. "Your mother, too. It's very important."

"Okay," I said. "Hang on."

Mom had just walked into the kitchen.

"It's Mr. Lukeman," I said. "He says he needs to talk to all of us really soon. It's important."

Mom looked puzzled, and she took the phone

from my hand and placed it to her ear.

"Hello, Mr. Lukeman."

There were several short pauses. "Yes," Mom said. "Okay, sure. I have lunch from noon until one. If we come by then, will that be okay?"

There was another pause as Mom listened to Mr. Lukeman's response.

"Fine," Mom said. "We'll see you then." She hung up the phone.

"What does he want to talk to us about?" Shannon asked.

Mom looked puzzled. "He didn't want to say. He said he wanted to speak to all of us, and that it was very important."

Well, we'd find out that what Mr. Lukeman needed to tell us certainly was important . . . and horrifying.

12

Mom returned from work and picked us up at the house. We were now in the car, making the short drive to *Waters of Wonder Scuba Shop*.

"I wonder what Mr. Lukeman needs to talk to us about," I said.

"I don't know," Mom replied. "But he sounded concerned about something. You guys haven't gotten into any trouble, have you?"

I shook my head. "No," I said. "Nothing I can think of."

"Me, neither," Shannon said from the back seat. "I'm a perfect angel."

"Yeah, right," I said as I rolled my eyes.

Mom turned the steering wheel and pulled into the dive shop's parking lot. Mr. Lukeman's car was there, parked next to a couple of the shop vans, which were colorfully decorated with pictures of happy scuba divers and fish. The shop logo was plastered on the sides of the vans, advertising the business. There were also several other cars, and one of them was a white truck. On the passenger door was a round logo, the size of a basketball. It had some strange design I'd never seen before and the words *International Seascape Laboratories* beneath it. I'd never heard of it before.

We walked into the dive shop. Kevin, one of the workers, was behind the cash register, cleaning some equipment. A couple of customers were looking at gear in a corner.

Kevin looked up and smiled when he saw us. "Hey, guys," he said. "Everyone's waiting for you in Mr. Lukeman's office."

Who is 'everyone?' I wondered. I thought Mr. Lukeman wanted to talk to us. Now, it seemed like a few people were in on it . . . whatever 'it' was.

We strode to the back of the store. Mr. Lukeman's office door was closed, and I rapped on it with a single knuckle.

The door opened. Mr. Lukeman stood, smiling thinly. Behind him, seated at a long, rectangular conference table, were a man and a woman. Both were dressed sharply, wearing business suits.

This is just getting weirder and weirder, I thought. *What do they want to talk to us about? Did we accidentally do something that might have gotten us into trouble?*

"Welcome," Mr. Lukeman said to us, and his voice was disarming. It wasn't the voice of someone angry or unhappy, and I felt relieved. Whatever he wanted to talk to us about, I was sure we hadn't done anything wrong.

"Thank you for coming," he continued. "This won't take long." He glanced at Mom. "And thank you, too, Mrs. Brenner. I know this is your lunch hour, and you're very busy." He gestured toward the table and three empty chairs.

"Please, have a seat," he said. "I'll introduce everyone, and we'll explain what this is all about."

We sat, and even before Mr. Lukeman began

speaking, I knew what he was about to tell us wasn't good. It was just one of those feelings I had, and I'd felt it ever since his phone call earlier in the day. I was sure that something was very, very wrong.

And I was right.

13

Mr. Lukeman made introductions. The man was Dr. Felding, a research scientist at *International Seascape Laboratories*. The woman, Dr. Pirelli, was a certified Master scuba diver from a professional dive company.

"Dr. Pirelli is an oceanaut," Dr. Felding explained. "She has actually lived in the ocean in special, underwater dwellings, performing scientific experiments for our organization."

Dr. Felding explained their dilemma: off the coast of Oregon, several miles out to sea, one of their research submarines called the *Deep Blue* had foundered and sank. Everyone had been able to get out safely, but the *Deep Blue* sank to the bottom of the sea. It now rested in ninety feet of water.

If that wasn't enough of a problem, the submarine developed a crack in the hull, filling the sub with water.

Worse: a canister in the submarine, containing a chemical called TNE-1, was slowly leaking. This chemical was very toxic and, if it wasn't removed, could threaten all ocean life for miles and miles.

"What is TNE-1?" Mom asked.

"TNE-1 stands for Tarconeal Nucleatic Epoxy," Dr. Felding replied. "It's an experimental, putty-like chemical we designed at our laboratory. It's mixed with a special resin to create a powerful, waterproof glue. When the putty and the resin are mixed together and applied, it isn't harmful. However, the putty alone is incredibly toxic in the water. In the water, the putty breaks down and gives off a thin, green gas that can travel miles and miles in the ocean."

"Is it killing the fish?" I asked.

Dr. Felding frowned, folding his hands on the table. "In time, yes," he said. "In time, the chemical will kill not only fish, but all marine life in a large area. Our divers have been to the submarine, and we know from underwater tests that the canister containing the TNE-1 has broken. The leak appears to be very slow, but it's enough to cause some disturbing effects to aquatic animals."

"What kind of disturbing effects?" Mom asked.

"First of all," Dr. Felding replied, "the chemical is very sweet-smelling to fish and other marine life, and it's attracting them from great distances. Animals that would normally not be found off the Oregon coast are attracted to the smell of TNE-1.

"Not only that," Dr. Felding continued "but the chemical is causing marine life—fish, in particular—to become very aggressive. I'm afraid if something isn't done soon, these conditions will only worsen. If we don't retrieve the canister and remove it from the ocean, all marine life for miles around will ultimately die. This could possibly grow to be the biggest oceanic catastrophe the Pacific has ever seen."

"But what do *we* have to do with this?" Shannon asked. I had been wondering the same thing.

All of this sounds terrible, I thought. *But why are they telling Shannon and Mom and me about it? What did we have to do with it?*

Dr. Pirelli spoke. "We've looked at all recovery options," she said. "If we raise the sub, we risk damaging it even more and possibly rupturing the chemical container and spilling all of the TNE-1. That would be disastrous."

"We have sent oceanauts down, including Dr. Pirelli," Dr. Felding said, "but the sub is resting on the escape hatch. The only way into the sub is through the rupture in the hull. That's where the TNE-1 is leaking out."

"Which brings us to the reason you're here," Mr. Lukeman said, nodding to me and Shannon. "A normal diver—an adult—is too big to slip through the crack in the hull. But a smaller diver—someone of your size—would be able to do it. Someone your size would be able to get into the sub and bring the container of TNE-1 to the surface."

A knot formed in my stomach. "But if it's a toxic chemical, what will it do to us?"

Dr. Felding shook his head and spoke. "Nothing," he said, "as long as you don't swallow any of it. You'll be breathing air normally through your regulator, so it will have no effect on you."

"Will it be dangerous?" Mom asked.

"As with any undersea mission of this sort," Mr. Lukeman replied, "there are always risks involved." Then, he nodded toward Shannon and me. "But with all of their training, with all the diving they've done, I know they could do it. They haven't been trained in shipwreck penetration, but I could take them through the course, in the pool. I've watched both of them become excellent, cautious divers. I know they could do this."

"What will happen if they don't?" Mom asked.

Mr. Lukeman's face became ashen. "We have no choice, I'm afraid. We need small divers to get into the sub. We might be able to find some other scuba divers that are your age, but none that are as small or nearly as skilled."

The room was silent for a long time, and the quiet became uncomfortable.

"Mrs. Brenner," Mr. Lukeman finally said as he looked at Mom. "I *know* your son and daughter can do this. We wouldn't be asking this if I wasn't completely certain. We desperately need their help."

I thought about all of my dives, and all of the marine life I'd seen, and how the ocean was such a wonderful, magical place. Then, I thought about all the animals and plant life dying.

We can do this, I thought. *We can stop that from happening.*

"We can do it, Mom," I said, looking at her. Then, I looked at Shannon. "We have to help."

Shannon nodded. She looked worried and maybe even a little scared, but I knew she agreed with me.

"We need your permission, Mrs. Brenner," Dr. Felding said. "We don't have a lot of time."

Shannon and I looked at Mom. Mom looked at me, then my sister.

"All right," Mom said.

Several emotions suddenly surged through my body: fear, exhilaration, nervousness, excitement. But my dive training brought everything back to normal, back into control, and self-confidence took over.

Operation Deep Blue Rescue was about to begin.

14

As Shannon and I slowly descended into the ocean, I recalled everything that had happened since our fateful meeting with Mr. Lukeman, Dr. Felding, and Dr. Pirelli. All of the training, the instruction from scientists and oceanauts at International Seascape Laboratories, all of our preparation had been for this moment, for this important dive: a mission to retrieve the container of TNE-1 from the *Deep Blue* and bring it safely to the surface.

Since the meeting, when we'd first found out

about the wrecked submarine, we'd learned a lot. I had asked Mr. Lukeman why they didn't just send down some welders and make the fissure wider, big enough for an adult to get through. He told me that the leaking chemical was flammable and that an underwater welding torch might ignite the gas, causing a huge explosion. I asked about a robotic arm to reach inside and retrieve the canister, but he said it was located too deep within the sub, and no mechanical arm could reach in that far.

And we also learned something else: within the past forty-eight hours, marine life around the toxic leak had begun to exhibit strange behavior. A large grouper, nearly three hundred pounds, had attacked one of the International Seascape Laboratories's rescarch ships that was on the surface, preparing for our mission. The huge fish didn't cause any damage, but the incident caused great alarm, simply because groupers are normally docile, calm fish. The one that had attacked the ship had gone mad, battering at the metal hull with its snout.

Closer to the coast, a swimmer had reported that a school of small fish had chased her in the shallows. The fish were only eight to ten inches long and didn't have any teeth, but the event had scared her out of the water.

"It's only a matter of time," Dr. Felding told us, shortly before our dive. "We must complete this operation as soon as we can, before more marine life becomes affected and before people start getting hurt by the animals . . . or worse."

We'd traveled several miles out to sea on one of the lab's dive boats, the *Sea Falcon*. Mom stayed behind to wait on the shore, because the boats were already crowded with necessary crews. Several other small boats from International Seascape Laboratories had joined us. They all dropped anchor and began final preparations for our mission. Earlier, a portable, two-person dive bell had been lowered to the ocean floor, not far from the submarine. Mr. Lukeman and Dr. Felding were inside, where they would be able to look through round portals and watch our progress.

I had been given the charge of carrying a small dive bag containing a flashlight and other tools necessary to remove the leaking canister of TNE-1. It also contained a 'lift bag,' which would be used to bring the heavy container to the surface without us having to carry it. Lift bags are great for bringing up heavy objects from the bottom of the ocean. All we would have to do was place the canister in the lift bag's pouch and use a regulator to inflate the bag with air. The bag, filled with air, would become a balloon of sorts. It would rise to the surface, carrying whatever contents the diver had affixed to it. Some lift bags are capable of bringing up objects weighing a thousand pounds!

I looked below us, into the depths. Several cables stretched from the *Sea Falcon* on the surface to the dive bell at the bottom of the ocean floor.

But we wouldn't be alone in the water, as Dr. Pirelli was joining us on our dive. She had to make some mechanical adjustments to the outside of the dive bell, and then she would join us at the submarine to monitor our efforts and help out if we somehow got into trouble. She would also help us with the lift bag, to make sure the canister of TNE-1 made it safely to the surface.

We won't need her help, I thought confidently as Shannon and I continued to descend into the depths, following the dark cables. Above us, on the surface, Dr. Pirelli had entered the water and was beginning her descent. *We're not going to get into trouble. Everything is going to go just as planned.*

Of course, nothing *ever* goes as planned, as I was only seconds away from finding out . . . when a large, moving shadow appeared below us.

15

Shannon and I froze. Beneath us, something big had passed by. It was too far away to see what it was, but it was easily as large as an adult. All we could make out was its dark, fuzzy shape. It vanished as quickly as it had appeared.

Shannon looked at me. Through her mask, I could see the worry in her eyes. I nodded, gave her the 'okay' sign with my thumb and forefinger, indicating that everything was all right, that we were going to be fine.

Just a curious fish, that's all, I told myself.

I pointed down, motioning to continue, and we continued our slow descent, careful to equalize as we went. Because the atmospheric pressure around you changes the farther you dive, it's necessary to adjust your own body pressure. This is done by simply holding your nose while gently trying to blow out. Some people can equalize by simply wiggling their jaw from side to side. Either way, it's important to do when you're scuba diving.

In ten minutes, this will be over, I thought. I exhaled smoothly, and bubbles gurgled as they were expelled by my regulator and rose to the surface. *It will only take us a few minutes, and we'll be heroes. We might even be on television. People will know us as the two kids who helped save the ocean.*

The only thing we would have to do on this dive was make what's called a 'decompression stop.' When you dive to deeper depths, air molecules get smaller. As you ascend, the air in your blood begins to get bigger and can form bubbles if you rise too quickly, leading to a painful condition called decompression sickness or 'the bends.' Air bubbles can become trapped in the joints of your body and really hurt. To keep this from happening, divers who attain deep depths of more than ninety feet will make several decompression stops on the return to the surface. A stop was nothing more than a pause in the ascent, usually about five minutes. Then, the ascent would continue. Depending on how deep the diver went, or how long he was at a certain depth, would determine how many stops would be made on the return to the surface. We wouldn't be diving more than ninety feet, but we would make one decompression stop, just to be safe.

Slowly, we glided deeper and deeper, kicking easily, propelled along by the smooth motion of our fins. Small fish appeared, looking at us as though we were alien invaders. Which, of course, we were. The undersea world belonged to them. We were simply guests, paying a short visit.

I turned, looked up, and saw the shape of Dr. Pirelli. Beyond her, the surface glowed like an aluminum plate. Rays of sunlight penetrated through the water, creating a shimmering, curtain-like effect. The boats moored above were only long, dark shapes, black blobs blotting the silvery surface like storm clouds.

Shannon had slipped a few feet beneath me. Like me, she had become an experienced diver. Although I didn't hang around my sister much at school or anywhere else, diving was something we both loved, something we did as a pair. We were a team, and I trusted her in the water. In scuba diving, that's important. You have to trust your dive partner with your life.

With a couple of harder kicks, I caught up with Shannon. Side by side, we continued our descent, following the cables. Our plan was to reach the dive bell, where we would be able to see Dr. Felding and Mr. Lukeman inside. If everything was going okay, we would signal them to let them know. The foundered submarine was only forty feet from the bell, and we had calculated that it would take about ten minutes to complete the entire mission.

Below, the dive bell came into view, along with the crippled submarine. Shannon and I continued to float downward, effortlessly. The mission was going just as smoothly as we planned.

And that's when something to the right of me moved.

At first, I thought it was just another fish, as

they were all over the place. But when I turned my head, I realized this wasn't an ordinary fish . . . it was a salmon shark, and he was cruising right toward us.

16

My left hand had been gently holding one of the cables as we descended, and I quickly let go and grabbed Shannon's arm. She turned her head and saw the huge salmon shark approaching. We both froze.

Salmon sharks are common in the Pacific, feeding mostly on salmon, which is how they got their name. They are usually dark gray or black with blotchy, light gray or white bellies. They don't grow nearly as big as great white sharks, but they can get as long as nine or ten feet. And, while they aren't known for attacking humans, they are certainly big enough to be a threat. The one slowly coming our way was seven or eight feet long—big enough to cause trouble if he wanted to.

I glanced up. Dr. Pirelli was too far away to do anything to help us, even if she could. In fact, she was looking up toward the surface and didn't even see what was going on below her.

Quickly, I unsnapped my dive knife on my leg and held it in my hand. Shannon and I both carry a knife, like many scuba divers. A dive knife is rarely, if ever, used as a weapon. It's simply a tool that has many uses and can be very helpful. For instance, you can get the attention of another diver by tapping the knife blade on a rock, or you can use it to poke and dig in sand, clay, or silt. I used my knife often during our dives.

But this time, I wasn't taking any chances. My dive knife was now a weapon, and it was the only defense I had against the huge shark heading toward us.

As the dark beast drew near, I could see its upper and lower rows of jagged, triangular teeth. I knew they were razor-sharp and could tear through our wetsuits and flesh as easily as a hot knife through butter. His eyes were like two shiny, black golf balls. Here, in the sea, this creature was afraid of nothing. We were in the salmon shark's kingdom, aquatic trespassers in his watery realm.

I felt Shannon stiffen in my grasp. It was pointless to try to swim away, to get out of the shark's path. He was much faster and far more powerful than my sister and me. If he wanted to attack us, he would, and the only thing I could hope to do was have my knife ready. A sharp poke on his snout might cause him to change his mind if he thought we were going to be his afternoon snack.

Thankfully, a fight was avoided. The salmon shark, for whatever reason, turned to his right. He swam past only a few feet away, his dark body easing through the water like a fleshy submarine. Shannon and I remained motionless, hanging in the water, while we watched the fish disappear into a gauzy curtain of blue.

I realized that my heart was pounding, and my breathing was deeper and heavier, which meant that I was using more air than was necessary.

Take it easy, I told myself, and I took slower,

calmer breaths. *The danger has passed. That's probably the last time we'll see that shark. We're nearly halfway through our mission, anyway. Soon, we'll be back on the boat, with the container of TNE-1 safely on board, no longer a threat to the ocean or marine life.*

We continued our descent, slowly making our way toward the dive bell, not realizing that the salmon shark was only the first of many threats we were about to encounter.

17

We reached the bell, a dome-shaped module the size of a large van. It rested at the bottom of the sea on a carpet of sand. To our right, the crippled sub loomed. Fifty feet above us, Dr. Pirelli was continuing her slow descent.

There were several round windows around the bell. In one of them, we saw the familiar faces of Mr. Lukeman and Dr. Felding. They looked out at us curiously, wondering. Shannon and I both gave them the all-okay signal. They looked noticeably relieved when they saw that we were all right. I didn't know if they had seen the salmon shark, but that didn't matter. The fish was gone, I was sure, and we had more important business to take care of: namely, bringing the canister and its harmful chemical to the surface.

Shannon met my stare through her mask, and I pointed toward the submarine. She nodded, and we started to swim toward it, a few feet from the ocean floor. Our fins kicked up grains of sand and silt, forming thin, vaporous clouds that mushroomed and bloomed.

As we drew closer, we found that the submarine was bigger than it looked from above. It was probably twice the size of the *Sea Falcon*. From where we were on the ocean floor, the submarine towered over us. It was resting near several formations of rocks and coral. Several plants grew nearby, wavering in the slow current, and the scene seemed calm and serene.

But I knew that what we were seeing was very deceiving. At first, we couldn't see any hint of the toxic TNE-1 spewing into the ocean, but as we got closer, there was a greenish, algae-colored mist that was rising above the sub, dispersing in the water.

And one thing we could see quite clearly: the

deep, angry rupture in the hull of the sub. The closer we got, the more apparent the green toxin became, drifting from the fissure like smoke from a smoldering campfire.

We stopped at the base of the sub, staring up at the large crack in the side of the hull. Shiny air bubbles jettisoned from our regulators and rose toward the surface, tangling and bouncing, billowing and rolling.

There's no way we're going to fit through that thing, I thought, looking at the scar on the sub. *The opening is way too small. We'll never be able to get inside.*

I glanced around, wary that the salmon shark might return. He was nowhere in sight, which was a relief. The last thing we needed was to have to deal with a crazed shark. Thankfully, the only fish I saw were small.

Forty feet away, Dr. Pirelli had reached the dive bell and was making some adjustments to a side panel. A string of air bubbles rose above her, making their lazy climb to the surface.

Shannon was staring up at the sub, and I knew she was thinking the same thing I was. I waved my arm in front of her mask to get her attention, and she turned. I hiked up my thumb.

Up?

She touched her thumb and forefinger.

Okay.

I pressed a valve on my buoyancy vest, filling it with just enough air to help me rise without having to kick hard with my fins. Shannon did the same, and we drifted like floating angels, following the hull of the sub, until we reached the crack.

Okay, I thought, after I had taken a closer look. *Maybe one of us could get through there, after all. But not while wearing all of our gear.*

The only way one of us would be able to make it through the crack was to slip out of our vest—which meant our air tank—and crawl through the crack. Then, the vest and tank could be pulled through and put back on again. Difficult, yes, but not that dangerous. Shannon and I had both done drills like that in the pool and in the ocean, except we were in much shallower water. The exercises were designed so we would learn how to remove our equipment, if necessary, to make an emergency ascent.

I pulled my flashlight from my gear bag, clicked it on, and shined it through the crack. A beam of light glanced off the interior of the submarine, illuminating metal and steel. When the light passed through the leaking chemical, the beam turned pea-green.

But then the beam lit up something I hadn't expected.

Eyes.

And a snout.

Before I had any indication of what I was seeing, of what had been lurking in the sub, the creature attacked.

18

The moment was over in a split-second. A wolf eel had been in the submarine, and the only thing Shannon and I could do was watch as the long, tube-like creature shot past us. We had been lucky, as we had probably scared the creature as much as he'd scared us. He'd been surprised when the light caught him, and he shot out of the crack like a lightning bolt.

Strange, I thought. *Wolf eels aren't normally found this far north in the Pacific.*

But I remembered what Dr. Felding had told us,

about how the TNE-1 was sweet-smelling to animals, attracting marine life from great distances, sea creatures that wouldn't normally be native to the area. Wolf eels aren't supposed to be dangerous to humans, but they'll bite if you don't leave them alone. I was glad the one we surprised wasn't in a biting mood.

I shined the light through the crack again, sweeping it around to make sure we wouldn't find any more sea life waiting to jump out at us. There was nothing to see except the interior of the submarine and the equipment.

Turning around, I looked at the dive bell. Dr. Pirelli was still working at the panel on the side. Although I could barely make out Dr. Felding and Mr. Lukeman through the round window, I gave them the all-okay sign. I was sure they had seen the big eel emerge from the submarine, and I wanted to let them know that Shannon and I were fine.

I turned back around.

We can do this, I thought.

I unclipped the dive bag attached to my waist and handed it to Shannon. At first, I don't think she knew what I was doing. But when I began to slip out of my BC vest, she understood.

It took only a moment to remove the vest. I had to be careful, as I needed to keep the regulator in my mouth to breathe. The regulator, of course, was attached to the hose that connected to the tank on my vest, so I had to be careful not to let go of it. Which was going to be a little tricky, because I had to worm my way through the crack in the hull to get inside the sub, all while having the regulator in my mouth and holding my vest with one hand.

Shannon helped by keeping a hold of my vest, making sure that, if I let go, she'd still have it.

Five minutes, I thought. *That's all this is going to take. In five minutes, we'll have the canister filled with TNE-1 in the lift bag, and it will be rising to the surface. We'll make one decompression stop during our ascent, and our mission will be complete.*

I reached through the crack in the hull with my left hand, being careful to watch for sharp, jagged edges that might tear my wetsuit or my vest. Or my regulator hose, like what had happened to Shannon. The last thing we needed was to have something like that happen and have to abandon the mission.

I pulled myself sideways, wriggling my body through the small opening. It was a tight fit, but I was going to make it. If I were on dry land, without all my diving gear, slipping through the same opening would be a cinch. Here, at the bottom of the ocean with all my bulky equipment, things were trickier.

Slow and easy, I told myself. Things were going fine. All I needed to do was take my time, be careful, and nothing would go wrong.

I was now almost completely inside the submarine, except for my right leg. Cautiously, I began to pull it through. Already, I had begun to think about what to do next.

Pull my vest through the crack, and put it on. Make sure it's secure.

I looked at Shannon, at her eyes through her mask, and I could tell that she was smiling, even with her regulator in her mouth. I was glad she was with me. We'd become good dive partners, a good team, and that was important . . . especially when it came to an important and dangerous mission like this one.

She still had a hold of my vest and my dive bag. I began to pull my vest through the thin fissure, where I would slip into it and begin the hunt for the leaking canister. Dr. Felding had told me it had been located in a refrigerator inside the sub's small, on-board laboratory, but it was thought that the fridge had broken open. The canister might be on the floor.

But it would still be tough for me to find, as I was unfamiliar with the inside of the submarine. Plus, it would be totally dark, and I would need to rely on my flashlight.

My vest and tank were almost through the crack. I was breathing easily, using my right leg for balance, pressing it against the fissure to hold me in place, when I spotted a movement over Shannon's shoulder.

The wolf eel.

He was swimming slowly toward us, inching through the water like a dark, fat snake.

Shannon caught my stare and realized I was looking at something beyond her. She turned . . . just as the eel opened its mouth and came at us.

19

Shannon made a fast move with my dive bag, and that's what saved her from a horrible bite. She swung the bag up, putting it between her and the eel. The eel's teeth sank into the mesh bag. But because the bag was made of strong nylon, it didn't tear. The creature quickly retreated, but it wasn't done yet.

This is crazy, I thought. *Eels don't attack people unless they're provoked.*

Again, I reminded myself about what Dr. Felding had told us, about how everyday, ordinary marine life would become increasingly aggressive because of the toxic chemical leaking into the ocean.

But how aggressive? I wondered. *And how many sea creatures would be affected?*

The eel came at us again, but Shannon was able to use the dive bag to divert his attention. The creature spun around and backed off, but still remained a few feet away, watching us, leering at us. Its eyes had a crazed, dazed look in them.

It's the chemical, I thought. *That's what's making him this way.*

And I felt sorry for him and other sea life that might be affected by the TNE-1. Although the eel and other creatures like him might become aggressive and attack us, it wasn't their fault. Most marine life simply want to be left alone, which is one of the reasons scuba diving is so exciting. It's fun to see the creatures in their own environment, going about their day. It's fun to learn from them and learn about them.

I was now more determined than ever to make our mission a success, to bring the canister and its deadly chemical to the surface before any permanent damage was done to the ocean and the marine life within it.

Shannon handed the dive bag to me, and I found a metal spike on the inside of the sub, a short knob that I could use as a hanger. I hung the bag on it and continued to work my vest and tank through the crack.

Meanwhile, Shannon had removed her dive knife from its sheath strapped to her leg, and she held out the blade, showing it to the eel, as if to say, *See? See what I got? I don't want to use it, but I will.*

The wolf eel remained several feet away, suspended in the water as if hanging by an invisible thread. He watched us for a moment before swimming slowly away. Shannon's head turned from side to side, then up and down, looking for the eel or any other creature that might threaten.

Finally, I succeeded in pulling my vest through. It was cumbersome and bulky, but I managed to slip into it easily enough and fasten the clips. I grabbed my dive bag, pulled out the flashlight, and turned it on. Then, I checked my gauges. I still had over seventy percent left in the air tank, which was easily enough to complete the mission.

Shannon turned and looked at me through the crack in the hull. She was still holding the knife in front of her, wielding it like a sword. She wasn't taking any chances, and I didn't blame her.

At the dive bell, Dr. Pirelli had finished her work. She was now on her way toward us, and I felt a sense of relief. Although I didn't think we would need her help, it was good to have her with us, especially because of the way some of the marine animals were acting.

I gave Shannon the all-okay sign. Then, I pointed into the submarine, indicating that I was on my way to hunt for the canister. She nodded, then turned away, a guardian of the submarine, on the lookout for eels, sharks, or any other creature affected by the effects of the TNE-1.

Holding the flashlight in front of me, I began to swim with slow, easy kicks, propelling my way into the *Deep Blue*. My movements were slow and deliberate, confident and controlled. There was no rush; I had plenty of time. Hurrying would only create problems.

Haste makes waste, is what my mom always told me. Meaning that the more you rush, the more likely your chances of making a mistake . . . and mistakes can't happen when you're in ninety feet of water, swimming inside a sunken submarine.

Just go easy, I thought. *I have plenty of air and plenty of time.*

Unfortunately, that was going to change.

20

As I made my way slowly through the *Deep Blue,* I thought more and more about how the direction of my life had changed within a year. Just last year, I'd had dreams of growing up to be a computer programmer or a software inventor. Now, those dreams had changed. The ocean was my home, the undersea world was what I dreamed of. I dreamed of working for Mr. Lukeman full-time, of traveling the world and taking customers on exciting dive vacations. I dreamed of exploring ancient shipwrecks and doing what I was doing at that very moment: using my skills for something good. And, as I made my way through the tight quarters of the submarine, I was proud of myself. I was glad Shannon and I were able to help. The success of this mission was up to us, and we had a big responsibility. We couldn't fail, and we wouldn't.

Diving within the confines of a shipwreck or any closed-in space can be dangerous. With Mr. Lukeman, Shannon and I had explored the remains of some old wrecks to practice for our mission. When you're under water and in close quarters, you have to be very careful, since years and years of silt has collected. If you move too fast or kick too hard with your fins, the silt gets stirred up, causing a 'silt out,' a thick cloud that makes visibility impossible. A diver can easily get confused and lost within a ship. If the diver gets lost, he can easily use up all of his air trying to find a way out.

Inside the *Deep Blue,* however, I didn't have that problem. There was no silt to kick up, and with the aid of my flashlight, visibility was clear, except for the greenish haze caused by the leaking TNE-1. Plus, the submarine was nowhere near as big as some of the shipwrecks we'd explored. Dr. Felding and Mr.

Lukeman said that the canister would be easy to find, and there was no danger of getting lost.

I slowed and looked behind me. I could no longer see Shannon, as I'd made a turn and was going through a narrow hallway. The sub was tilted to the side, and a number of things had been displaced and knocked over when it sank to the ocean floor. Dr. Felding said that losing the *Deep Blue* was going to cost International Seascape Laboratories more than eight million dollars. And I thought it was expensive when I broke our neighbor's living room window with a softball last year!

All the while, my flashlight beam glowed green as it penetrated through the leaking chemical. I was heading in the right direction, and I knew I'd find the canister soon. Everything was going exactly as planned. Maybe even better.

My heart sank as I made the turn to enter the submarine's on-board laboratory. The entry was blocked by an enormous piece of equipment that had tumbled sideways. It looked like some sort of large, metal filing cabinet with double doors, and I didn't have to look twice to know that there was no space big enough for me to wiggle through. I had no choice: to get into the room and get the canister of TNE-1, I'd have to move the cabinet.

I placed the flashlight on the floor and aimed the beam at the cabinet. Then, I stood with my fins flat on the floor. Reaching out, I tried to push the cabinet. It didn't budge, not even an inch. I knelt down and tried to lift it. Again, no luck.

I looked through my dive bag to see if my tools would be of any use. There were some smaller items like pliers and scissors, but nothing that would help to move the huge cabinet.

I moved back, taking a moment to think.

What I really need is something I can use as a lever, I thought. I picked up the flashlight and swept the beam around, looking for a pipe of some sort. A fine green mist seemed to hang all around me in the water.

Above, I found exactly what I was looking for. There were rows and rows of pipes stretching along the corridor. One of them had been damaged in the fall, and it had broken off at one end. I grabbed it with one hand and pulled, moving it back and forth, side to side. Finally, it broke off.

Returning to the cabinet, I again placed the

flashlight on the floor. The beam was a misty, green color from the chemical leaking from the lab. I took the pipe, wedged it beneath the cabinet, and pushed it down.

It took all the strength that I had, but the cabinet began to move. I kept pressure on the bar, pushing, pushing—

Suddenly, the bar went limp as the cabinet made a huge shift. The problem now, of course, was that the cabinet was falling in my direction, and there was no way I'd be able to get out of its way in time.

I tried to swim to the side, to cover my head with my hands, but it was too late. The cabinet came crashing down on top of me and smashed my flashlight. The beam of light went out.

I tried to move my legs, but I couldn't. My arms were pinned, too.

I was trapped in a submarine, beneath a cabinet, ninety feet from the surface, in total darkness.

21

I was in big trouble, and I knew it.

Nothing I'd ever been through in my life prepared me for the horror, the overwhelming feeling of helplessness that I was experiencing at that very moment. It was a terror I'd never felt before. Sure, everyone at one time or another is afraid of the monster in the closet or the creature under the bed, and everyone gets spooked by scary movies now and then.

But this was something completely and totally

different, as I knew that there was a very good possibility that I wasn't going to make it out of the submarine alive. Sure, the cabinet had made some noise when it came crashing down, but sound doesn't travel under water the way it travels above the surface. I was sure that Shannon and Dr. Pirelli wouldn't have heard it.

Keep cool, I told myself. The only chance I had was to try to stay calm and figure a way out of the mess I was in.

I quickly made a mental list of my biggest problems:

A heavy cabinet has fallen on me.

I can't see a thing.

I can't move.

I have a limited supply of air.

No one knows I'm trapped, and even if they did, they can't get to me.

Yep . . . things were about as desperate as they could ever get.

I found that I could wiggle my left leg, but my right leg was pinned, along with both of my arms. I was thankful that the fall hadn't knocked the regulator from my mouth, as I would never have been able to reach it to put it back. Without my regulator, I could hold my breath for about a minute . . . and then it would be all over for me.

I managed to wriggle my left arm free. My elbow hit something, and I grasped at it.

My flashlight.

Amazingly, it hadn't been smashed after all, and when I flipped the 'on' switch, the light bloomed. The fall had knocked the switch to the 'off' position, but the unit hadn't been damaged. That alone was a small miracle, and I allowed a little bubble of hope to grow.

If I can just get my legs and my other arm free, I thought. I continued to struggle, trying to remain calm and not exert too much energy, which would cause me to breathe heavier, faster, and deeper, using too much valuable air.

Finally, I was able to get my other arm free. Now, all I had to do was get my legs free, and that was going to be tricky. The full weight of the cabinet rested on them. My left ankle was a little sore, but I hardly noticed it. I was just thankful that the cabinet hadn't broken any bones when it crashed down on me.

I put the flashlight aside, placed both hands on the cabinet, and pushed. I succeeded in raising it a tiny bit, and I was able to move my legs. But the cabinet was heavy, and I couldn't hold it up for very long. I let it back down, rested for a few seconds, then tried again. This time, I was able to wiggle my legs even more, working them back and forth, side to side. The fins made motion difficult, as they were pinned under a corner of the cabinet.

I rested again, then tried once more. This time, I succeeded. My left leg came free, then my right. I pulled away, rolling on my side, back from the cabinet. When my legs were safely away, I let go of the cabinet. It crashed to the floor.

I did it! I thought. *I'm going to make it out of here, after all!*

My small bubble of hope had mushroomed, growing into a huge balloon of exhilaration. Not only had I pulled myself out of a terrible situation, but I'd succeeded in moving the cabinet away from the doorway to the submarine's laboratory. I now had clear access to the submarine's lab, and I was sure I would find the leaking canister and complete *Operation Deep Blue Rescue*. After all: what else could go wrong?

The answer?

Everything.

Everything that *could* go wrong *would* go wrong. If I thought I'd had my share of trouble already, I was in for a rude awakening as to how bad my problems could really get.

22

I looked at my gauges. I'd used a lot of air while I was pinned under the cabinet, and I was now down to forty percent. Still, I had enough air to safely make it back to the surface.

I picked up my flashlight and aimed the beam into the sub's laboratory. The light glowed deep green as it swept through the leaking chemical.

Slowly kicking my fins, I swam forward, drifting over the cabinet and through the doorway to the lab, sweeping the flashlight back and forth from wall to wall.

The laboratory was a mess. Many items had fallen, and pieces of paper wavered in a gentle, unseen current. And everywhere I pointed the flashlight, the beam glowed bright green. All I had to do was locate the source: the leaking canister. Then, I had to do nothing more than put it in my dive bag, exit the sub, place the canister in the lift bag, and let it rise to the surface where the rest of the team was waiting to retrieve it. Then, Shannon, Dr. Pirelli, and I would begin our ascent to the surface.

I found the canister easily enough. It was in a large refrigerator, just like Dr. Felding had said.

But that was the problem. The fridge had fallen sideways, the door had opened, and the edge of it had jammed into the wall. The opening was only a few inches wide, and this was where the TNE-1 was coming from. If the refrigerator hadn't opened during the accident, there wouldn't have been a leak, even if the canister had broken open.

I searched my dive bag again, but the tools it contained weren't going to be of much use. I had a pair of pliers that were strong, but they wouldn't help get the door unstuck.

No problem, I thought. I wasn't going to let myself and the mission fail because of a jammed refrigerator door.

I turned and swam back to the doorway, found the pipe I'd used to jimmy the cabinet, and returned to the fridge. I put the flashlight on the floor, placed the end of the pipe in the door, wedged it sideways, and pulled.

No luck. The door was really jammed into the wall. It wouldn't budge an inch.

I stepped closer, shining the light into the fridge. On the bottom shelf, a silver can the size of a milk gallon was on its side. There was a very small puncture near the bottom, and a bright green gas-like substance boiled out.

That's it? I thought. *That little leak from that small can is causing all of this trouble?*

Still, I remembered what I'd been told: that TNE-1 was highly toxic. In the canister, it was putty. But when it mixed with water, it became a gas, capable of filtering miles and miles into the ocean.

But how can I get to it? I thought. *How do I get the refrigerator door open, so I can get to the container?*

I tried another tactic, placing the metal pipe

119

lower, near the floor. I was able to use the bottom of my fins, placing the weight and pressure on my heels, while my air tank was pressed against the wall, giving me a little more leverage.

I pushed, and the pipe bent a little. I pushed harder, and the door budged. I kept pushing, harder still, until the door finally gave way and snapped off its hinges. The refrigerator never moved as the door tumbled to the side. Now, I had easy access to the leaking canister.

I picked up the flashlight, reached into the fridge, and pulled out the can, which was much heavier than I'd expected. Green gas continued to spew into the water and swirl all around me. I was glad I didn't have to breathe in any of the stuff.

So, this is what's causing all the trouble, I thought, as I put the canister into my dive bag. *Not anymore. We'll have the canister and the TNE-1 out of the ocean in no time at all.*

I began swimming, carrying the bag in one hand and the flashlight in the other. It was difficult, as the canister was heavy. Normally, I could just clip my dive bag to my vest and not have to hold it, but not with such a bulky container inside of it. I was glad I had the lift bag, as it would be awfully hard to carry the canister to the surface on my own.

Still, I managed. I just swam slowly, kicking my fins easily as I drifted through the water-filled laboratory. The mission was as good as over. We'd succeeded.

And I don't know why I hadn't thought of this before, but it never occurred to me that there might be other marine life inside of the *Deep Blue*. I guess I had thought that since we'd scared away the wolf eel, there wouldn't be anything else in the submarine besides small fish.

Well, I was about to find out in the worst way that I was wrong. I should have known better, and I should have been more cautious . . . because something was waiting around the next corner. It was a creature of massive size, and I'd never before encountered one on any of my dives.

And the leaking TNE-1 had affected this marine animal in horrible, horrible ways. When I saw the monstrous beast blocking my exit, I realized I'd made an awful mistake. Lurking in the corridor of the submarine and preventing my escape was what is known as the deadly *Diablo Rojo*.

The red devil.

Or, known by a more common name:

The giant Humboldt squid.

23

My luck had run out, and I knew it.

Humboldt squids grow to enormous sizes. Their bodies alone can measure over five feet, and with their long tentacles, they appear much bigger. Normally, they live in very deep water, which is why it's rare for divers to see them. I was sure that the leaking TNE-1 had attracted the squid from the deep, and it found the perfect hiding spot in the dark depths of the submarine. Its unique shape and flexibility probably allowed it to easily slip through the crack in the sub's hull.

Although Humboldt squids are thought to be passive, they can become nasty and mean during times of feeding. They have eight tentacles, each with over 1,000 sucker discs. Each disc has several dozen razor-sharp ring teeth. Their mouths aren't really mouths at all, but super-sharp beaks, like that of an eagle. Plus, they can move fast in the water, at speeds over twenty miles an hour. In short: they're a deadly undersea killing machine, if they want to be.

Now, here I was, face-to-face with the terror of the Pacific, the Diablo Rojo, the Red Devil, the giant Humboldt squid, staring me down in the belly of the *Deep Blue*.

I didn't dare take the beam of light away from him, as I wanted to be able to see where he was. At the moment, he didn't appear to be threatening, but he took up the entire passageway. He must have been in another part of the sub when I came through the first time. Maybe he heard the commotion I was making and came to investigate.

Whatever the reason, I wasn't getting past him . . . and there was no other way out of the sub. He might not even attack me, either. He could just stay where he was, and I would be forced to try to get past him or remain where I was until he moved . . . or until I ran out of air.

I didn't have many options, and none of them were very good.

Mom always says there's a solution to every problem, if you just think hard enough. She's right, of course. Sometimes, the solution isn't what you want it to be, but it has to be done if you want to get yourself out of a jam.

And what a jam I was in at the moment! There was no way I could contact anyone for help, no way to let anyone know what I was up against. I could try tapping on some metal in the sub, and Shannon or Dr. Pirelli might hear it, but what could they do?

The giant squid slowly began to move toward me, crawling along on his tentacles, drifting like an eight-legged ghost.

I had no choice. I had to move. I had to act. My life depended on it.

I thought of every option I had, and there was only one thing I could try. It was risky, and it might not work, but it was the only thing I could do.

All right, I thought. *Here goes . . . .*

24

Slowly, I began to back away from the squid. My plan was to backtrack toward the lab, turn off the light, and lay face down on the floor. I would remain there, motionless, and hope that the creature would crawl over top of me and not even know I was there.

The tricky part, of course, would be that I would have to hold my breath. The moment I let it out, bubbles would expel through my regulator, and he'd know exactly where I was.

On top of that, Humboldt squids usually remain

in deep, dark water, and their eyesight is very good. If I moved an inch, he would see it.

But if I could stay very, very still and hold my breath . . . .

This is crazy, I thought as I backed farther and farther into the sub. *This will never work.*

The squid continued to come toward me, but he didn't seem to be in any hurry. That gave me some time to put some distance between us. When I reached the laboratory, I shut off the flashlight. Then, I released a little air from my buoyancy vest to make me sink a little bit, which would allow me to remain on the floor without worrying about drifting up.

I placed my dive bag next to me, but I never let go of it. Nor did I let go of the flashlight in my other hand. I stretched out as flat as I could, took one deep, long, last breath . . . and held it. In my mind, I began to count steadily.

One . . . .

My personal record for holding my breath was just over one minute. After one full minute, I didn't think I'd be able to hold my breath any longer.

I continued counting, waiting, motionless.

Eleven . . . .

Something touched my arm in the darkness, and I almost flinched. It crawled along my wrist and up to my elbow.

Twenty-nine . . . .

Another touch, this time on my other arm. Soon, giant tentacles were grasping at my suit and my vest. The creature was pulling itself along, making its way through the sub. I was under him, and he was actually on top of me, touching my wetsuit. It was a creepy feeling, like there were insects crawling all over me.

Forty-one . . . .

I could feel that familiar tightness in my lungs, telling me to exhale, to breathe. But I couldn't. The squid was still on top of me.

Forty-eight . . . .

The squid was still moving, and he was now crawling along my lower legs.

Fifty-two . . . .

My lungs began to burn.

Fifty-three . . . .

The last of the tentacles released their grip. The squid had passed over me, not even knowing I was there.

Fifty-seven . . . .

My lungs were on fire, but I knew that the eight-legged beast was still close by. It was too soon to move.

Sixty-one . . . .

I couldn't take it any more. I needed to exhale, I needed to breathe.

In a single motion, I exhaled, turned on the flashlight, and kicked my fins. This wasn't a time to remain calm and cool . . . this was the time to get away as fast as I possibly could. I didn't look back, I didn't turn my head. I focused on the beam of light in front of me, of swimming through the dark corridor, of the sub, carrying my dive bag with the canister of leaking TNE-1. Of course, I'd still have to worry about getting through the crack in the hull, but I'd figure that out . . . if I made it that far.

Suddenly, the flashlight beam dimmed and the light faded. It was as if the batteries were dying, and fast.

Then, I realized it wasn't the flashlight that was the problem . . . it was the water. It was darker, muddier. It was like I was suddenly swimming in a vat of dark chocolate. Black smoke was suddenly swirling all around me.

Then, I realized what had happened. The giant Humboldt had shot a blast of ink, which is what they do to confuse their prey or disorient an attacker, so the squid can make a getaway. The thick, black cloud of smoke enveloped all around me in the corridor, making it nearly impossible to see where I was going.

I had tricked the squid once, but he was going to see to it that I didn't do it again.

25

If the squid shot the cloud of ink to confuse me, it was working. I was disoriented, all right. I could still see the beam coming from my flashlight, but it was almost impossible to see where I was going.

And where was the squid? Was he coming after me? Had I merely surprised him, and he shot the blast of ink thinking he was in danger?

None of that mattered at the moment. What mattered was that I had to get away. I had to keep moving, to paw my way along the corridor, until I found the fissure in the side of the *Deep Blue* and slipped out of the sub with the canister of TNE-1 and began our ascent to the surface.

I scrabbled clumsily along the corridor, blindly, making my way through the chalky, swirling ink. I bumped into the floor, the walls. My dive bag with the leaking canister smacked against my leg. My air tank on my back banged into unseen objects.

The murky ink began to thin as I made my way through the sub. That little bubble of hope that had grown and shrank, grown and shrank, returned. Once again, I started to think that maybe—just *maybe*—the mission was going to be a success. Maybe I would make it out alive, after all.

Still, I had no idea where the squid was. He could be right behind me, ready to attack, and I'd never know it.

But I couldn't think about that right now. I needed to stay focused on moving, on getting out of the sub and beginning our ascent to the surface. If the squid attacked, there really wasn't anything I could do about it.

Then, up ahead, through the clearing water, I saw something.

A bar of light. The crack in the hull of the sub.

I'm going to make it! I thought. *I am! I'm going to make it out of here!*

I continued to swim toward the exit, mentally preparing myself for what I would need to do.

Hand my flashlight and dive bag to Shannon and Dr. Pirelli. Take off my vest and push it through the crack. Wiggle out. Put my vest back on. Put my flashlight in the bag. Begin our rise to the surface.

I reached the crack, expecting Shannon and Dr. Pirelli to be waiting, but I didn't see them. They must have been just out of view, on either side of the crack.

I hung my dive bag on the same piece of metal I'd used before and poked my head through the crack.

Shannon and Dr. Pirelli were gone.

26

It was just another problem added to a list that was getting longer moment by moment.

Where could they be? I wondered. All sorts of thoughts began to spin through my mind.

Did the salmon shark return? The eel? Something else?

I turned and looked behind me, shining my flashlight into the submarine to see if the squid was coming. When I didn't see him, I immediately began to plan.

Hang the bag with the leaking TNE-1.

Put down the flashlight.

Slip out of my vest.

I would have to hold onto my vest while I squeezed through the crack in the sub, then pull it through, put it on, then grab my dive bag and my flashlight. Then, I would search for Shannon and Dr. Pirelli. I was certain they couldn't be far from the sub.

Unless there was some sort of emergency, and they had to ascend, I thought.

No. They wouldn't leave me. I knew that Shannon, as my dive partner, would never leave me, and I wouldn't ever leave her.

I made one more quick glance into the sub, just to be sure the squid wasn't coming after me. I didn't see him.

Quickly, I hung the dive bag. However, in doing so, I was a little clumsy with the flashlight. It fell, bounced off my knee and out the crack, where it tumbled to the ocean floor some twenty feet below.

No matter. I really didn't need it anymore.

Holding my vest and tank so they wouldn't drift away, I began to wriggle through the crack in the hull of the submarine. It was harder this time, since I didn't have both hands to work with. Still, I managed, and soon, I had my right leg and my right arm through.

Still holding my vest and tank, I continued to wiggle and squirm.

Almost there, I thought. *Everything is fine. Shannon and Dr. Pirelli are fine. There must be some reason why they had to move away.*

I continued to struggle, but not forcefully. I stayed calm and worked easily, careful not to exert more energy than necessary. The air in my tank was already low, and I didn't want to use up more than I had to.

Focused on my escape and holding my vest, I never even saw the wolf eel as he came from the depths and latched onto my right arm above my elbow.

27

The attack was so sudden and unexpected that I nearly screamed into my regulator. Instinctively, I let go of my vest and tank, so I could use my free arm to fend off my attacker . . . who happened to be Shannon.

I let out a huge sigh through my regulator, glad that I wasn't getting chomped by the wolf eel. Or worse: the salmon shark.

Dr. Pirelli was behind Shannon, drifting weightlessly in the water, kicking her fins very slowly. I had no idea where they had been, but I sure was glad they'd returned. I was sure they'd explain later.

I turned, grabbed my vest and tank, and pulled them through the crack after I'd finally succeeded in slipping through. Shannon helped me back into my vest and tank. When it was secured, I reached through the crack in the sub, found the bag containing the canister, and pulled it through. I passed the entire bag to Dr. Pirelli.

We did it! I thought. *We got the canister!*

I turned to look at the dive bell, and I could make out the shapes of Mr. Lukeman and Dr. Felding in one of the circular windows. I was sure they were excited, as well as relieved.

Now, all we had to do was attach the lift bag to the dive bag, fill it with air, and let it rise to the surface on its own. There, it would float until it was plucked from the waters by one of the crew members above.

I looked at my gauges. I'd used a lot of air, but I still had enough to complete my ascent to the surface with one decompression stop. We hadn't really dived deep enough to worry about getting the bends, but we were deep enough that it would be good to make at least one decompression stop, just to be on the safe side.

We watched as Dr. Pirelli removed the leaking canister of TNE-1 and the lift bag from my dive bag. She unfolded the balloon and attached the bag containing the canister to the lift apparatus.

Then, she removed the regulator from her mouth. Bubbles of air spewed from the mouthpiece, boiling upward to meet the surface some ninety feet above. When she held the regulator under the lift bag, the air rose into it, filling the bag like a balloon. It grew and grew until it began to rise on its own, carrying the canister of TNE-1 with it.

The three of us watched as the lift bag rose up, on its way to the surface. Even though we were at a depth of ninety feet, the water was clear, and we could make out the fuzzy, dark shapes of the boats on the surface.

But we also saw another dark shape.

This one was smaller than the boats, but it was still quite big. It cruised at mid-depth, about forty feet above us.

Still, I couldn't quite make out what it was. It was shaped too differently to be a shark, and it definitely wasn't the wolf eel.

But when it turned, there was no question as to

what we were seeing: a sailfish.

Sailfish are magnificent creatures. They are long and slender like most fish, but they have an enormous dorsal fin that extends from just behind their eyes all the way down their backs, almost to their tails. Their bodies can be different colors, but most are a bluish-silver color, as was the one we were looking at. Their giant dorsal fins are serrated and teeth-like and are a deep, dark blue. They also have a long, pointed nose that extends out like a spear. Sailfish are a popular gamefish, and they are sought after by many fishermen. In fact, Mr. Lukeman has a sailfish mounted on a wall in his dive shop.

I'd never seen one in any of my dives before. In fact, I wasn't aware that sailfish existed in the northern Pacific. I always thought they were found in the warmer, more tropical waters.

But I was once again reminded that Dr. Felding had told us that the TNE-1 would attract species of fish and marine life from great distances.

And he also said that the chemical would make some of the animals and fish become very aggressive, I thought.

The sailfish swam above us, circling the lift bag

and its contents. It seemed strangely fascinated and began circling faster and closer.

No, I thought. *He's not going to. He's not going to—*

I was becoming more and more worried that the sailfish wasn't simply curious, but crazed with anger. I was concerned that the TNE-1 was having some effect and that the fish might do something . . . either to one of us or the lift bag.

And this time, the lift bag would be the victim.

The sailfish stopped swimming and hung in the water as the lift bag continued its rise to the surface. Then, in one sudden, lightning-burst move, it shot forward and used its long, spear-like snout to tear a hole in the lift bag. The air spewed from the torn nylon, and the bag containing the canister began to sink back to the ocean floor.

28

While the sailfish posed no immediate danger, the situation it had caused would mean a change of plans. The bag containing the canister sank toward us faster and faster as the air in the balloon bubbled out. The sailfish now seemed bored and slowly swam off.

What next? I thought. While the problem we were faced with wasn't all that difficult, it just seemed like another annoyance piled on top of the things that had already happened.

The bag containing the canister drifted down

into the open and waiting arms of Dr. Pirelli, who grasped the failed lift bag. Then, she signaled to us, indicating that she was going to ascend. I was sure it would be more difficult now that she had to carry the canister, but after all, she was an experienced diver, an oceanaut. She was probably used to situations like this.

Shannon and I would also ascend, but we were going to swim to the dive bell where we could follow the cables up. It would be easier to make our five-minute decompression stop if we had something to hang onto.

I waved to Shannon, urging her to follow me as I swam toward the dive bell. She followed, and we stopped when we reached the large dome structure resting on the sea floor. Through one of the windows, we could see Mr. Lukeman and Dr. Felding. Both were smiling, and Mr. Lukeman hiked his thumb up and mouthed the words 'good job.' I returned the gesture with my own thumb, smiling through my regulator. Things were going as planned.

Swimming slowly, Shannon and I rose over the dive bell and reached the cables that extended to the boats on the surface.

A few small fish surrounded us, watching as we

ascended into the oceanic sky. Beneath us, the dive bell seemed to fall away as we put more and more distance between it and us.

I glanced at my gauges. We'd reached a depth of fifty feet, which was where we would make our decompression stop.

I relaxed and grasped a cable with my right hand. Shannon stopped swimming, and she, too, grasped a cable. I looked at my dive watch to mark the time. We would remain at a depth of fifty feet for five minutes to allow the air in our bloodstream to normalize.

Above us, Dr. Pirelli had finished a short decompression stop and was continuing her ascent. She was nearing the surface, carrying the dive bag containing the canister with her right hand. Her ascent had been slow and easy, unhurried . . . just the way all ascents to the surface should be.

One minute passed, and we had four minutes to go. I passed the time by looking around, watching fish, gazing into the depths, hoping I didn't see any sign of the wolf eel or the salmon shark. I would be glad when the mission was over, when we were out of the water and safely in the boat where we could talk about the dive.

But I'd forgotten all about the giant squid, thinking that he was probably still in the submarine.

I was about to find out differently.

29

At the two and a half minute mark, I signaled Shannon by clenching my fist once in front of her. This meant that we were at the halfway mark of our decompression stop. Her head nodded in acknowledgment. She looked eager, anxious to continue our rise to the surface, where, no doubt, we would receive a hero's welcome.

Suddenly, the expression in Shannon's eyes changed. She was now looking to the right of my shoulder and down. Her eyes grew wide and filled with horror, like the look she gets when I hide in her closet, jump out, and scare her.

I turned my head to follow her gaze downward, already knowing that something was coming. Something was threatening that was big and nasty—but I didn't expect it to be the giant squid. He must have slithered out of the *Deep Blue* the same way he'd gotten in: through the torn seam in the hull. Now, he was coming toward us, his long tentacles pushing him along.

And he was *fast!* I knew that giant Humboldt squids can swim very quickly, but I didn't realize just how speedy they are.

Of course, I'd never seen one in action before. I'd had one experience with the squid inside the submarine, and that had been bad enough. I'd barely escaped with my life. Now, Shannon and I both would have to move and think fast to keep the huge creature from having one of us as a midday snack.

I turned to Shannon and pointed up. We had no choice but to cut our decompression stop early and head for the surface as fast as possible. This was no time for a slow, casual ascent. This was an emergency, and we needed to get out of the water as quickly as possible.

We let go of the cables and began our rise to the surface, kicking our fins as hard as we could, keeping our mouths open to exhale. This was important, since the air in our lungs would expand rapidly during our hurried ascent. When this happens, you need to exhale to keep your lungs from becoming too filled with air and bursting.

Our focus became the boats above us, dark shapes against a flat, chrome surface. I knew that crews were waiting on those boats, ready to help us out of the water . . . I just hoped that we made it in time.

I shot a quick glance below. The squid was still coming as fast as ever. I turned my head upward and continued to kick as hard as I could.

My breathing became labored and difficult. It was hard to draw a breath, and when I looked at my gauges, I realized why.

I was still thirty feet from the surface—from safety—and I was completely out of air.

30

I had been so close.

Thirty feet above me, hope waited in the form of boats and crews ready to help. Thirty feet below me, a monster was charging.

Shannon continued to swim. She didn't know that my air was gone, but there was nothing she could do, anyway. If she remained with me so I could buddy-breathe from her regulator, we'd both be in danger of the squid attacking. She continued her ascent to the surface, rising above me.

I had only one chance, and I knew I had to act fast. I would have to slip out of my buoyancy vest, air tank, and weight belt, abandon them, and swim to the surface. Ditching those items would make me less cumbersome in the water, and I'd be able to swim quicker. Plus, without my heavy belt, tank, and vest, my wetsuit would help with buoyancy, and I'd make it to the surface even faster. The questions were: could I hold my breath long enough to reach the surface, and could I move faster than the giant squid?

I was about to find out.

I unsnapped my weight belt from around my waist and let it fall away, tumbling into the depths. Then, I slipped out of my vest and tank, letting them slowly sink to the bottom. I knew that the vest and tank were expensive, but I was sure that they could be salvaged by another diver. Besides: I wasn't going to worry too much about a weight belt, vest, and air tank when my life was being threatened by an enormous, eight-legged water beast.

Quickly, I unsnapped my dive knife and pulled it from the sheath. If the worst happened—and it might—I wanted to try to defend myself. Having a knife probably wouldn't do much good, but it was better than having nothing at all.

The gigantic Humboldt squid was still racing toward me, his long, tube-like body snaking through the water, propelled by his churning eight tentacles.

I turned toward the surface and swam with everything I had, careful to exhale tiny bubbles out of my mouth, so the air in my lungs wouldn't expand and cause a problem. I kicked with my legs, and I pulled with my left arm, but it was difficult to swim with my right arm since I was holding the knife. Still, the wetsuit made me much more buoyant, and I was able to move much faster than I had while wearing my weight belt, vest, and tank. I began to believe I was going to make it, after all . . . until I glanced down and saw the gargantuan squid only a few yards away. He had already turned and was preparing to lash out with his tentacles.

I was still fifteen feet from the surface, but now I had no choice. If I continued my ascent, the squid would easily overtake me. The only choice I had would be to turn and face the beast and hope that my knife would work. If the squid realized I was going to put up a serious fight, he might think twice before attacking. Maybe he wouldn't attack, after all.

There was a dull ache growing in my lungs, and I knew that I had only about thirty seconds before I would need air. In thirty seconds, I would have to fend off the giant squid and make it to the surface. It seemed like an impossible task.

The squid's tentacles reared back. The creature was sizing me up, wondering if I would be a threat, wondering if I was worth his effort.

Apparently, he wasn't going to be frightened off that easily, because he inched closer, threatening with his long tentacles. I could see the dangerous suckers on each one, and I knew they contained tiny, razor-sharp teeth that could easily tear me to shreds. I could see his eyes, watching me, glaring at me, burning with hatred.

I waved my dive knife, trying to show the squid that I was going to put up resistance, that I wasn't going to be an easy meal. If he was going to have me for lunch, he was going to have to work for it. I wasn't going down without a fight.

A tentacle lashed out, and I swiped at it with my knife. Missed. The creature withdrew for a moment, but lashed out again with the same tentacle. Again, I swung my knife, but I wasn't prepared for what the squid did next.

Using another tentacle, the creature lashed out and grabbed my wrist. I was able to pull away and free myself, but not before the squid succeeded in dislodging the dive knife from my hand. The shiny tool dropped, tumbling and spinning as it sank to the ocean floor.

I was fifteen feet from the surface, facing down a giant squid. I had no weapon . . . and I was out of air.

31

My lungs were on fire, and I knew I would never make it to the surface in time. Even if the giant squid backed off and left me alone, there was no way I'd be able to hold my breath long enough to make it to the surface.

A shadow above me caught my eye, and I looked up.

Two divers! Two divers had entered the water and were coming toward me!

One of the divers was an adult, and he was carrying a spear gun.

The other diver was Shannon!

The squid showed no signs of backing off. He remained where he was, tentacles poised and ready.

Shannon descended to where I was, while the other diver cautiously approached the squid, diverting the creature's attention. Now that I didn't have to worry about being eaten, I could concentrate on something else: getting air into my lungs.

Using my right hand, I made several quick slices at my neck, indicating to Shannon that I was out of air. She immediately took a deep breath from her regulator, pulled it from her mouth, and handed it to me. I put it in my mouth as I exhaled, then drew a long, deep, breath.

Air!

It felt so good to fill my lungs with fresh, clean air. I exhaled, took another breath, then repeated. Then, I drew one more breath, held it, and gave the regulator back to Shannon, who took several breaths before giving the regulator to me again.

The diver with the spear gun had managed to keep the squid's attention, drawing the animal away from us. When the squid lashed out, the diver poked it with the sharp tip of the spear.

162

That was all it took. The squid felt the jab, drew back, and hesitated for a moment before retreating. We watched him as he picked up speed and returned to the depths.

Shannon pointed up, and I nodded. Time to go home. Together, we ascended the final few yards to the surface, ready to emerge from the sea and bathe in the warm sunshine, safe at last.

But it wasn't going to be quite that easy. There was one more danger we'd have to face . . . and it came in the form of the most feared king of the ocean.

A great white shark.

32

Relief surged through my body as I broke the surface . . . until I saw the large fin approaching in the distance.

The shark hadn't been noticed by any of the crew members. They were lining the boats, clapping and applauding as we reached the surface, too excited about the success of the mission.

I pointed and yelled, *"Shark!"*

Heads turned, and the crew members sprang into action. Shannon and I swam frantically toward the closest boat, where a man and a woman waited to assist us out of the water.

"*Hurry!*" the man shouted.

I could tell by the frantic shouts on the boats that the crew members were worried. No one had seen the shark approaching, and now it was circling the boats, only several dozen feet from Shannon and me. We splashed and swam, harder and faster than ever.

"*You're going to make it!*" the woman shouted. "*Just a little more!*"

I reached the boat first. The man tried to grab my arms, but I pulled away and turned to help Shannon. Behind her, a huge fin rose up into the air. A fin that big would belong to a shark over fifteen feet long. Last year, I read a book about a giant shark called a Megalodon in a freshwater lake in Mississippi. That was a scary book . . . but it wasn't real. That fish was only in the author's imagination and in the minds of kids like me who had read the book. What was happening to us right now was as real as real can get.

Dimly aware of people shouting orders and scurrying among the boats, I grabbed my sister's left hand and pulled her to the boat, where the man and woman grabbed her and hauled her aboard. Shannon stumbled and nearly fell, but she was caught just in time by another crew member.

She made it, I thought. *Shannon is safe.*

But the great white was still coming, still barreling toward me like a toothy, undersea locomotive.

I reached up.

The man grabbed my left hand.

The woman grabbed my right.

But the great white was faster than I thought, and with a single, powerful lunge, clamped his enormous, teeth-filled mouth onto both of my feet.

33

The shark nearly pulled me from the grasp of the man and the woman, but another crew member came to my assistance, grabbing my arm and pulling.

It was a tug of war: two men and a woman against a giant, great white shark.

And oddly enough, I didn't feel any pain. I'd heard that sometimes during moments of high adrenaline and excitement, the rush of horrific pain is delayed. I knew when it came, it would probably be the most excruciating pain I'd ever felt in my life, knowing that the shark would have severed both of my legs just above the ankle.

Suddenly, I was free. The two men and the woman fell back as I came sprawling on board, tumbling and falling onto the deck. I rolled over, still not feeling any pain, but knowing it was going to come. I looked for the blood I thought for sure would be gushing all over the place.

No pain.

No blood.

But my fins . . . .

The great white had missed my foot by mere inches, clamping down on my fins until his teeth had cut through. The bright yellow fins had been destroyed, chopped off just beneath my toes.

Holy cow, I thought. Then: *When I go back to school in the fall, I hope I get to write about what I did on summer vacation. No one is going to believe this!*

The rest of the afternoon was a blur, a bustle of activity on all of the boats. The crew members shook our hands and congratulated us, telling us that we'd done a great job, that we'd saved the ocean from catastrophe. Shannon and I explained everything that happened to us on our dive, and I told everyone about getting trapped in the sub and outsmarting the giant Humboldt squid. Everyone listened eagerly, amazed and horrified, and again I thought what a great story I'd be able to write when I went back to school.

But I might not even wait until then, I thought. *I might just write the story on my own, for fun. I bet lots of people would want to read it. It might even be scarier than that book about the giant shark in Mississippi.*

The dive bell was raised, and Dr. Felding and Mr. Lukeman emerged and climbed aboard our boat. They congratulated us, and once again Shannon and I repeated our stories. After everything that had happened, after the dangers had been faced and we'd made it out alive, it turned out to be a good day.

And I was glad I was small for my age. Shannon and I had been able to help out, simply because we weren't as big as other kids who were as old as we were.

The following week, there seemed to be no end to the attention Shannon and I got from newspapers, television stations, and radio stations. We did lots of interviews and retold our stories dozens of times. We were heroes, sort of, although I didn't really feel like it. I felt like we'd just had an important job to do, and we did it. We succeeded.

And I hoped that we wouldn't have to go through something like that ever again. I hoped the rest of our dives would be for fun and pleasure. I wanted to experience the beauty of the ocean and the thrill of seeing different fish and marine animals. I didn't want to be faced with any more situations like we'd just gone through.

Then, one day, Mr. Lukeman called.

34

"He didn't say what he wanted?" Mom asked, moments after I'd told her that I had just spoken with Mr. Lukeman on the phone, and he wanted to see us at his shop.

Again.

Over a week had gone by since our dive to retrieve the canister of TNE-1. We were still getting calls requesting interviews, but the steady stream of phone calls and reporters at our door was dwindling.

"He didn't say," I said to Mom. She and

Shannon were in the kitchen, making cookies. "He just said that he'd like us all to come to his shop tonight at six o'clock."

"I wonder if he has another mission for you guys," Mom said. "After what happened last week, I'm not so sure I'm going to let you do something like that again."

I wasn't so sure I wanted to do that again, either. While I loved to dive, and I would always want to help if I could, our mission last week had been dangerous in ways we hadn't planned. Although we knew that the TNE-1 had affected some of the marine life, no one—including Shannon and me—had been prepared for how aggressive some of the creatures had become.

Now that the chemical had been removed from the water, though, it was thought that most of the fish and other aquatic animals had returned to normal. There was no evidence the toxic TNE-1 had permanently harmed anything in the ocean.

A few minutes before six that night, we piled into Mom's car and drove to *Waters of Wonder Scuba Shop*. There were several cars in the parking lot, including some television vans. About a dozen well-dressed people were outside, milling about. I saw two people holding big, black television cameras on their shoulders.

"I wonder what's going on?" Shannon said as we got out of the car. "Everyone is watching us."

"Probably another interview," I said.

I felt a little uncomfortable as we walked across the parking lot. All eyes were on me, Mom, and Shannon. But everyone seemed happy and smiling.

Maybe Mr. Lukeman really does have another mission for us, I thought.

No one said anything to us, which was kind of strange. They moved away as we approached the shop, smiling and nodding.

Odd.

Mr. Lukeman met us at the door. He was grinning as we walked inside.

"Welcome," he said. "Thanks for coming." He shook our hands. "I know you must be wondering why I've called you here, and I will say this right away: I don't have another mission for you." Then, he winked. "Not yet, anyway," he said.

I was confused. Why would he want to see us? Couldn't he have just told us what he wanted over the phone?

Shannon spoke. "Then, why are we here?" she asked.

"International Seascape Laboratories wanted to thank you personally for your brave efforts last week," Mr. Lukeman replied. "They have a special gift for each of you."

Cool! I thought. *We're going to get awards. Maybe plaques we can hang on our bedroom walls.*

"They are waiting for you in my office," Mr. Lukeman continued. "I've invited some news crews, because I thought they might want to interview you after you receive your gifts from ISL. Come this way."

We followed Mr. Lukeman to his office. He pushed the door open, and we went inside. There, Dr. Felding waited, along with Dr. Pirelli. On Mr. Lukeman's desk, dive equipment was piled: two new wetsuits, two masks, two pairs of fins, two air tanks, two vests, and other diving accessories and tools.

My heart beat faster.

That can't be for us, I thought.

"Congratulations once again on a job well done," Dr. Felding said. "We wanted to do something to show our appreciation for your successful mission and a job well done. In speaking with Mr. Lukeman, we decided that you both might like your own scuba diving equipment."

My mouth hung open in disbelief. I couldn't believe it! Shannon and I now had our very own scuba diving gear!

We stepped closer to the table and inspected the items, carefully going over the masks, fins, vests, and wetsuits. It was all very nice equipment. There would be no way I would be able to afford to buy anything like it on my own. Oh, I'd been saving my money, but I didn't have nearly enough to buy such nice dive gear.

"Thank you!" I suddenly blurted out.

"Yeah, thanks!" Shannon echoed.

Dr. Pirelli smiled. "No," she said. "The thanks goes to you two. Thanks to you, a disaster has been averted. On behalf of International Seascape Laboratories, we'd like to present you with your very own diving gear, along with these."

Dr. Pirelli and Mr. Lukeman reached down on the other side of the table where we couldn't see, and they each held up a large, shiny plaque.

"Now it's official," Mr. Lukeman said as he held out the plaque. I took it in my hands and looked at it,

Engraved on shiny brass were the words:

International Seascape Laboratories
Jacob Brenner
Honorary Oceanaut

Dr. Pirelli handed her plaque to Shannon, which was identical to mine except her name was engraved on it.

There was a camera flash and a click as someone took a picture, but I hardly noticed it. I was too excited, too focused on the diving equipment on the table and the plaque in my hands.

The rest of the evening was a flurry of interviews, a blur of cameras, and lots of handshaking. I really felt important and very proud. Shannon did, too, and I know Mom was proud.

Later, we loaded all of our new diving gear and our plaques into Mom's car and took it home. I laid everything out on my bedroom floor, going over it piece by piece, until nearly midnight. It had been an incredible week, and I was sure that Shannon and I were the only kids in America who'd ever had an adventure that had been so thrilling, yet so horrifying at the same time.

But I was wrong.

The very next day I met someone who'd had a similar experience. No, not scuba diving. She'd had the experience on land, and it had to do with ordinary household appliances.

Her name was Brooke Whipkey, and she was from Virginia. Her family had traveled to Portland for a family reunion, and she had joined in a game of basketball with my friends at the park. I didn't talk to her before or during the game, but when we took a break, she sat next to me at a picnic table. Her shoulder-length black hair shined in the sun. She smiled at me.

"You're that kid I saw on television," she said.

I nodded. I'd gotten used to people saying things like that to me over the past week.

"Yeah," I said.

"Did you really get attacked by a great white shark?" she asked.

"Yeah," I replied with a nod. "And other things, too. I was attacked by a salmon shark, a wolf eel, and a giant squid. But I was lucky, and I didn't get bitten by any of them. My fins sure got mangled, though."

"I wasn't so lucky, a few weeks ago," Brooke said.

I frowned. "What do you mean?" I asked.

"Well, I didn't go scuba diving," Brooke replied. "But I was attacked, just like you."

"By what?" I asked. "Wild animals?"

Brooke shook her head. "No," she said. "Vacuum cleaners."

I almost got up and walked away. Clearly, Brooke was out of her mind. She'd lost her marbles.

Vacuum cleaners can't attack people, I thought.

She must have read my mind, because she continued before I could say or do anything.

"I know what you're thinking," she said. "You're thinking that I'm crazy, and that vacuum cleaners can't come to life and attack. Well, if you'll give me a chance to explain, you'll realize I'm telling the truth."

"Go for it," I said. "I'm listening." I was sure she was going to begin by telling a fib bigger than the Empire State building, but I decided to listen, anyway. After all: it's not every day that you get to sit down and have a conversation with a person that's gone totally crazy.

Brooke began her story. I listened . . . and soon,

I realized that she wasn't making anything up. Brooke's horrifying ordeal had *really* happened. She wasn't crazy, and she wasn't making it up. In Virginia, vacuum cleaners had come alive . . . and what they did was absolutely *terrifying*.

Next:

America's #1 Series for MAXIMUM Chills!

#30: Vicious Vacuums of Virginia

Continue on for a FREE preview!

My name is Brooke Whipkey, and I live on Churchside Drive in Gainesville, Virginia, which is a city not far from Washington, D.C. In fact, that's where my mom works. She works at the White House as an assistant for a state senator. She loves her job, but she works late and she's gone a lot.

My dad is an architect, and he works out of his home office upstairs. He designs homes and buildings, and he's very good at it. He's even won some awards for his designs.

My uncle Chet, who lives only a few miles away, is also very good at what he does: repairing vacuums. He has a shop in a warehouse not far from where we live. He's a nice guy and one of my favorite relatives, but Dad says he's always been a little nutty, that he's always looking for ways to get rich quick. He has some good ideas, but they just never seem to work for him.

But my Uncle Chet's shop was where me and my friend, Spider Murphy, got into a *lot* of trouble. And by the way, his real name isn't 'Spider,' it's Bartholomew. He's named after his great-grandfather or something like that. But he doesn't like the name, and he doesn't want to be called 'Bart' for short. So, everyone calls him Spider. He said he's been called that ever since he was four years old. Personally, I don't care what anybody's name is. Spider is cool, and he's been a good friend for a long time. We like a lot of the same things, including one hobby, in particular:

Electronics.

Now, that might sound strange to you, but

not to me. Sure, some of the kids at school think I'm weird. They think I should be more like them. They don't think of electronics is a hobby that girls should like, but I do. I've loved electronics ever since I was little, when I accidentally received a kit as a gift from my grandparents.

I say 'accidentally' because that's exactly what it was: an accident. You see, my cousin Matt and I share the very same birthday . . . except he's two years older than me, and lives in Gainesville, Florida. Well, on my seventh birthday, my grandparents goofed. They sent Matt's present to me in Gainesville, Virginia, and my present to him in Gainesville, Florida. When I opened the box to find an electronics kit, I was really excited. I'd never seen one before, and I thought it was cool. It was very basic, but there were some neat things to build: a homemade radio, and a clock that was powered by an ordinary potato! I had a lot of fun.

But the funny part? My grandparents had bought me a talking doll and accidentally sent it to Matt. He was really confused as to why his grandparents would send him a doll.

When my grandparents found out what they'd done, they felt terrible. The plan was to swap gifts: I would send the electronics kit to Matt, and he would send the doll to me.

But I said no way. I had already opened the electronics kit, and I was having too much fun with it. I didn't even *want* the doll. In the end, Matt gave the doll to his little sister and my grandparents bought him what he *really* wanted: a skateboard. Everyone was happy . . . especially Matt's little sister, who got a present even though it wasn't her birthday.

But I think I was happiest of all. I had hours of fun with that kit, learning about electricity and how it worked. My parents bought me another kit, and soon I was making all kinds of experimental electrical things on my own. Most of the things I built were pretty basic, but I sure had a lot of fun. I even won first prize at our school science fair when I was only eight years old!

So you see, I've been fascinated with

electrical things for years. I'm still fascinated, of course, but now I tend to be a lot more careful . . . especially after something horrible happened one awful day in December.

When I got home from school that day in December, I was excited to see a package waiting for me. I'd saved up my money and ordered a burglar alarm kit. It was a pretty simple unit, but I thought it would be fun to build and hook it up to my bedroom door. That way, my brother Andrew would get the surprise of his life the next time he tried to sneak into my room. Andrew is two years younger than me, and he's nothing but a nosy pest. He is always getting into my room, going through my stuff, and just being a pain. I'd hoped my burglar alarm would catch him in the act.

As far as kits go, my burglar alarm was complicated. I'd already built quite a few electrical things—small, simple robots, lights, radios—things like that. The first ones I built were really easy and were made for beginners.

Since then I've built a lot of things, and I've learned a lot about electricity and how it works. Once, I was able to rewire Mom's broken blinker on her car. She was happy because she said that if she had to take it to the repair shop, it would probably have cost her a fortune.

So, I was always looking for more challenging kits and experiments. After a while, the really simple things get boring. I like challenges, and what I really wanted to do was enter a robotics competition. Not only that, I wanted to *win*. Which, of course, meant that I'd really have to know a lot about electronics.

By building my burglar alarm kit, I was sure I'd learn a lot. It was designed for kids aged fourteen and older, but I was confident that I could build it even though I was only eleven.

"I'm home, Dad!" I called out as I dropped my book bag on the couch.

"Did you find your package, Brooke?" I heard Dad reply from his upstairs office.

"Yeah!" I said.

"Mom called and said she's going to be late," Dad hollered. "That means I'll be making dinner tonight."

Which meant, of course, that he would call to order a pizza and have it delivered. Dad might be good at designing homes and buildings, but he can't cook worth beans.

But that was fine with me. I love pizza, and so does Andrew.

I picked up the package and carried it to my bedroom. Using my fingernail, I sliced through the packaging tape and carefully opened the box. Inside were the contents of the burglar alarm kit and an instruction booklet.

Spreading out everything on my desk, I got

to work, mindful that Andrew would be coming home from soccer practice soon. I didn't want him to see what I was working on, because that would ruin the surprise. After all, the whole purpose in having my burglar alarm was to give him the scare of his life when he came into my bedroom uninvited.

I worked at assembling the alarm. By far, it was the most complicated piece of electronics I'd built. But it was fun.

After working for over an hour, I was almost finished building the alarm. As I inserted the battery, I heard the front door slam. Andrew was home.

I got up to close my bedroom door so he wouldn't come in when the phone rang. I closed my door behind me, walked into the kitchen, and picked up the phone. It was Spider. He had some questions about his math homework. Spider is pretty smart, but sometimes he just doesn't pay attention. I told him that if he actually listened to our teacher and read his textbooks, he'd be able to figure out the work on his own.

We chatted for a while before I hung up. Andrew had dropped his book bag on the floor and was seated on the couch watching television, and Dad was still upstairs, working. It was four-thirty. In about an hour, he would call down for me to order a large pizza, and Andrew and I would fight over what toppings we wanted.

I walked down the hall and stopped.

Something smelled funny.

I pushed open my bedroom door . . . only to find the entire room filled with smoke!

Panic surged through my entire body. My skin felt hot. My entire room was filled with a cloud of gray smoke.

I quickly saw that my burglar alarm on my desk was the cause. It wasn't on fire, but smoke was rising up, and it looked like it was about to erupt in flames.

Fanning smoke away from my face, I hurried to my desk. Using a screwdriver so I wouldn't burn my fingers, I pried the battery from the unit. I was sure that I had made a mistake in the wiring and when I had put the battery in, the unit short-circuited.

But now I had another problem.

The smoke had drifted into the hall and set off the smoke alarm. The high-pitched squeal made me jump, and I raced out of my bedroom.

"False alarm, Dad!" I called out. "No need to come downstairs! I'll get it!"

I hurried into the kitchen, grabbed a chair from the dining room table, and carried it into the hall. I stood on it, reached up, and removed the battery from the smoke detector. It immediately ceased its loud, shrill beeping.

I just have to remember to put the battery back in, I thought. To make sure I would remember, I left the chair in the hall and put the battery on it.

Then, I went into my room, closed the door, and opened the window. Cold, wintry air swept in, chilling my skin and swirling the curtains.

Maybe I can get all the smoke smell out before

Dad or Mom or Andrew finds out, I thought hopefully. Not that I would get into any trouble, but there wasn't any need for them to know I could have started the house on fire with my miswired burglar alarm.

Which was another problem. My burglar alarm was fried. The wires were blackened, and the unit's casing was charred. I was sure it was ruined.

I was disappointed, but I realized it could have been much worse. If I'd spent another five minutes talking to Spider, the unit might have burst into flames and set my room on fire. That would have been a disaster.

From that day forward, I decided that whenever it came to electricity, I would be extra careful . . . no matter how simple the project seemed. Electricity isn't something to play around with, and it can be extremely dangerous.

But I never knew how dangerous and terrifying it could be until the following summer at my uncle Chet's vacuum cleaner repair shop.

ABOUT THE AUTHOR

Johnathan Rand is the author of more than 65 books, with well over 4 million copies in print. Series include **AMERICAN CHILLERS, MICHIGAN CHILLERS, FREDDIE FERNORTNER, FEARLESS FIRST GRADER**, and **THE ADVENTURE CLUB.** He's also co-authored a novel for teens (with Christopher Knight) entitled **PANDEMIA**. When not traveling, Rand lives in northern Michigan with his wife and three dogs. He is also the only author in the world to have a store that sells only his works: **CHILLERMANIA!** is located in Indian River, Michigan. Johnathan Rand is not always at the store, but he has been known to drop by frequently. Find out more at:

www.americanchillers.com

ATTENTION YOUNG AUTHORS!
DON'T MISS

JOHNATHAN RAND'S

AUTHOR QUEST

THE DEFINITIVE WRITER'S CAMP
FOR SERIOUS YOUNG WRITERS©

If you want to sharpen your writing skills, become a better writer, and have a blast, Johnathan Rand's Author Quest is for you!

Designed exclusively for young writers, Author Quest is 4 days/3 nights of writing courses, instruction, and classes at Camp Ocqueoc, nestled in the secluded wilds of northern lower Michigan. Oh, there are lots of other fun indoor and outdoor activities, too . . . but the main focus of Author Quest is about becoming an even better writer! Instructors include published authors and (of course!) Johnathan Rand. No matter what kind of writing you enjoy: fiction, non-fiction, fantasy, thriller/horror, humor, mystery, history . . . this camp is designed for writers who have this in common: they LOVE to write, and they want to improve their skills!

For complete details and an application, visit:

www.americanchillers.com

Johnathan Rand travels internationally
for school visits and book signings! For
booking information, call:

1 (231) 238-0338!

www.americanchillers.com

Other books by Johnathan Rand:

Michigan Chillers:
#1: Mayhem on Mackinac Island
#2: Terror Stalks Traverse City
#3: Poltergeists of Petoskey
#4: Aliens Attack Alpena
#5: Gargoyles of Gaylord
#6: Strange Spirits of St. Ignace
#7: Kreepy Klowns of Kalamazoo
#8: Dinosaurs Destroy Detroit
#9: Sinister Spiders of Saginaw
#10: Mackinaw City Mummies
#11: Great Lakes Ghost Ship
#12: AuSable Alligators
#13: Gruesome Ghouls of Grand Rapids
#14: Bionic Bats of Bay City

American Chillers:
#1: The Michigan Mega-Monsters
#2: Ogres of Ohio
#3: Florida Fog Phantoms
#4: New York Ninjas
#5: Terrible Tractors of Texas
#6: Invisible Iguanas of Illinois
#7: Wisconsin Werewolves
#8: Minnesota Mall Mannequins
#9: Iron Insects Invade Indiana
#10: Missouri Madhouse
#11: Poisonous Pythons Paralyze Pennsylvania
#12: Dangerous Dolls of Delaware
#13: Virtual Vampires of Vermont
#14: Creepy Condors of California
#15: Nebraska Nightcrawlers
#16: Alien Androids Assault Arizona
#17: South Carolina Sea Creatures
#18: Washington Wax Museum
#19: North Dakota Night Dragons
#20: Mutant Mammoths of Montana
#21: Terrifying Toys of Tennessee
#22: Nuclear Jellyfish of New Jersey
#23: Wicked Velociraptors of West Virginia
#24: Haunting in New Hampshire
#25: Mississippi Megalodon
#26: Oklahoma Outbreak
#27: Kentucky Komodo Dragons
#28: Curse of the Connecticut Coyotes
#29: Oregon Oceanauts
#30: Vicious Vacuums of Virginia

Freddie Fernortner, Fearless First Grader:

#1: The Fantastic Flying Bicycle
#2: The Super-Scary Night Thingy
#3: A Haunting We Will Go
#4: Freddie's Dog Walking Service
#5: The Big Box Fort
#6: Mr. Chewy's Big Adventure
#7: The Magical Wading Pool
#8: Chipper's Crazy Carnival
#9: Attack of the Dust Bunnies from Outer Space!
#10: The Pond Monster

Adventure Club series:
#1: Ghost in the Graveyard
#2: Ghost in the Grand
#3: The Haunted Schoolhouse

For Teens:
PANDEMIA: A novel of the bird flu and the end of the world
(written with Christopher Knight)

American Chillers Double Thrillers:
Vampire Nation &
Attack of the Monster Venus Melon

Dont Miss:

WRITTEN AND READ
ALOUD BY JOHNATHAN
RAND!
AVAILABLE ONLY ON
COMPACT DISC!

Beware! This special audio CD contains six bone-chilling stories written and read aloud by the master of spooky suspense! American Chillers author Johnathan Rand shares six original tales of terror, including *The People of the Trees, The Mystery of Coyote Lake, Midnight Train, The Phone Call, The House at the End of Gallows Lane,* and the chilling poem, *Dark Night.* Turn out the lights, find a comfortable place, and get ready to enter the strange and bizarre world of **CREEPY CAMPFIRE CHILLERS!**

ONLY 9.99!
over sixty minutes
of audio!

Order online at
www.americanchillers.com
or call toll-free: 1-888-420-4244!

Join the official

AMERICAN
CHILLERS

FAN CLUB!

Visit www.americanchillers.com for details!

Browse the official
American Chillers website!

AMERICANCHILLERS.COM

Order books, read sample chapters
for free, and see thousands of
pictures and videos from
Johnathan Rand's
travels!

5.7/4

All AudioCraft books are proudly printed, bound, and manufactured in the United States of America, utilizing American resources, labor, and materials.

USA